REWIND

SANDI LYNN

Sandi Lynn Romance, LLC

Rewind

Copyright © 2019 Sandi Lynn Romance, LLC

Cover Photo & Design by Sara Eirew Photography

Editing by BZ Hercules

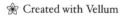 Created with Vellum

MISSION STATEMENT

Sandi Lynn Romance

Providing readers with romance novels that will whisk them away to another world and from the daily grind of life – one book at a time.

Quinn
The summer I turned seventeen was the year when my life changed forever.

"Smile." I grinned as I held up my camera.

"Quinn, you've taken enough pictures of me." Noah smiled as he playfully put his hand up.

"I could never have enough pictures of you."

I snapped one last picture and set my camera on the bench in Central Park. I looked into his eyes as a sadness swept over me.

"We're going to make it, right?"

"Come here, baby." He pulled me into him and held me tight. "Of course we're going to make it. We already have our entire future planned out. I'm only going to be three hours away and I'll be home every single weekend and you'll be coming to visit me. Before you attend Yale, you'll already know the campus." He kissed the top of my head.

"I'm going to miss seeing you every day. It's going to be so hard."

"I know." His grip around me tightened. "It's going to be hard on me too, but we'll facetime every single day. It's only for a year and then we'll be with each other again. We'll get an apartment together, study together, and that year we were apart will be as if it never happened. I love you, Quinn Stevens. You are my heart and soul and I will always love you to the moon and back."

"I love you too, Noah."

"I have something for you." He smiled as he reached into his pocket, pulled out a light blue box and handed it to me.

I smiled brightly as I stared into his eyes, feeling nothing but love and happiness. Opening the lid, I gasped as I saw a beautiful silver heart-shaped locket with a diamond in the middle.

"Noah, it's beautiful," I spoke as I took it from the box.

"Open it up."

I slowly opened the locket that was engraved on the inside.

I will always love you to the moon and back.

"Oh, Noah." Tears filled my eyes.

"This is my heart, Quinn, and even when we're apart, I want you to remember that you'll have it and that I'll always be with you."

He took the necklace from my hand and placed it around my neck. Our lips met each other's in the middle of Central Park as the clouds rolled in and the rain started to pour down on us.

"Oh my god." I laughed as I looked up at the sky.

"I have an idea. Come on." He grabbed my hand and we started running toward Greyshot Arch. "We'll stay under here until the rain stops."

We stood under the arch, shielded from the rain that had already soaked us. Noah Kingston was my knight in shining armor. He was my world and my very existence. We met when I had just turned sixteen and I was in Kingston's, the high-end department store his family owned in Manhattan. I was shopping with my mom, when my purse accidentally knocked over a very expensive glass vase. I wanted to die of humiliation as everyone turned and stared at me. When I bent down to clean up the mess I made, an unfamiliar hand gripped itself around my wrist to stop me from touching the glass. When I looked up, the only thing I saw was bright beautiful blue eyes staring into mine.

"I'll call for someone to clean that up. I don't want you to get hurt." He smiled and something unfamiliar tore through me.

"I'm sorry. I can be such a klutz sometimes."

"It's fine. It was an accident. Just like this was." He took his hand and knocked over a glass vase onto the floor as he gave me a wink.

I couldn't believe he just did that. He helped me up, let go of my wrist, and extended his hand.

"I'm Noah Kingston."

"I'm Quinn Stevens." A smile crossed my lips as I placed my hand in his.

"It's nice to meet you, Quinn."

"Your last name is Kingston? As in the store?"

He chuckled. "Yes, my family owns it. I was just passing by on my way up to the fourth floor, when I heard the glass break."

"Again, I'm sorry. I feel so stupid," I spoke as I could feel the heat rise in my cheeks.

"Well, you can make it up to me." He grinned.

"And what is it you want me to do?" My brow arched at him.

"You can agree to have dinner with me tonight."

"Really? You want to take me to dinner?" I bashfully asked.

"I do." The smile on his face grew wider.

Even though I had just known him a mere few seconds, I already felt like I'd known him forever. There was something in his smile that made me feel warm and safe. We had dinner that night and hadn't been apart since. Even though we both attended different schools, we saw each other every single day. In a couple of weeks, he'd be going off to Yale while I stayed behind and finished high school.

࿐

"Looks like the rain stopped. I better get you home in time to go to dinner with your parents," he spoke as he softly stroked my hand.

"I wish you could come with us." I pouted.

"I do too. I would rather spend the evening with you guys than go to that board of directors meeting with my dad."

"I still don't understand why you have to go."

"Because it's my future and I'm going to be running the company one day." His lips softly brushed against mine. "But don't worry. I'll be thinking about you the whole time."

"And I'll be thinking about you the whole time at dinner."

When Noah pulled up to my house, my parents walked out the front door.

"Sorry I'm late," I spoke as I climbed out of the car.

"That's okay, sweetheart," my dad said. "Hey, Noah. Can you take a picture of the three of us?" he asked as he held up his new polaroid instant camera that my mom had bought him as an anniversary gift.

"Sure, Mr. Stevens."

The three of us hooked our arms around each other and smiled as Noah snapped the picture.

"Thank you, son." My dad smiled as he took the picture and camera from him. "I'm going to put this in the house. You two say your goodbyes. I don't want to be late for our reservation."

My parents walked inside the house and I walked over to Noah and wrapped my arms around his neck. Our lips met as he gave me a long kiss goodbye.

"Have fun at dinner tonight." He placed his forehead against mine.

"Have fun at your board meeting."

"I love you to the moon and back, Quinn Stevens."

"I love you too, Noah Kingston."

2

oah

I loved that girl more than life itself. She was my world, and even though we were young, I already knew we'd be together forever. I'd do anything for her and I knew she'd do anything for me. From the moment her baby blue eyes stared into mine at the department store, a spark flared inside me that I'd never felt before. I was breathless, and I knew right then and there, she was the one I was meant to be with for the rest of my life.

***

I WAS IN THE MIDDLE OF THE BOARD OF DIRECTORS MEETING, listening to my father go over the last quarter sales, which had increased by thirty percent over the quarter before, when I felt my phone vibrate in my pocket. When I glanced at it, I didn't recognize the number, so I slipped it back in my pocket. Once the meeting was over, I pulled my phone out to text Quinn, and I noticed I had a voicemail.

"Hello, this is Mount-Sinai's Emergency Department calling. Your number was listed as the emergency contact for a Miss Quinn Stevens. We need you to

come to the Emergency Room immediately. We will answer all questions when you arrive."

A sickness tore through me as my heart started racing.

"Dad, I have to go. I need you to have Sean drive me to Mount Sinai. Something happened to Quinn."

I ran out of the building and climbed into the back of the limo. I kept trying to call her parents, but they weren't picking up.

"Sean, I need you to drive faster!" I shouted.

"Noah, I'm trying," he replied.

I could barely catch my breath at the thought that something bad happened to her. I tried her parents again, and yet, there was still no answer from either one of them.

"I received a call regarding Quinn Stevens," I spoke in panic as I ran to the nurses' station. "I was her emergency contact."

"Come with me," the nurse with the dark hair and dark eyes spoke. "Her parents had their phones locked and no emergency contact listed. We were lucky that Quinn had you in her phone."

She led me into a room and told me that a doctor would be in to speak with me shortly. I paced around the room, back and forth with my hands tucked tightly into my pockets. My stomach was in knots and my mind was filled with fear and worry.

"Are you here for Quinn Stevens?" An older man in blue scrubs walked in.

"Yes. I'm Noah Kingston. What happened to Quinn and where is she?"

"Mr. Kingston, please have a seat." He gestured to the chair.

"I don't want to have a seat. I want to know where Quinn is!" I raised my voice.

"Okay. Calm down, please. Quinn and her parents were in a terrible car accident. Quinn suffered some head trauma and a couple of broken ribs. She's up in surgery now."

"And her parents?" I asked.

"I'm sorry, but they didn't make it."

I stumbled into the chair and covered my face with my trembling hands.

"I'm sorry, Mr. Kingston. Our staff is trying to locate the family."

"I can give you the number for Quinn's grandmother." I ran my hands down my face.

◎◆◎

I WAITED IN THE SURGICAL WAITING ROOM UNTIL ONE OF THE nurses came and took me to Quinn's room. I swallowed hard as tears filled my eyes when I stood in the doorway and stared at her. I barely recognized her. Her head was wrapped in a white bandage, and her face was severely swollen and bruised. The room was filled with steady beeps from the machines she was hooked up to.

"Hi, I'm Doctor White. I'm the neurosurgeon who operated on Quinn."

"How is she?" I asked as I walked over to her bedside.

"She's in very critical condition and will be carefully monitored for the next twenty-four hours. There was a lot of swelling and bleeding in her brain, but I was able to stop it."

"So she's going to be all right?"

"We won't know until she wakes up, which could be in a couple of days. It's hard to tell. Everyone is different. I do want to prepare you for something else."

"What?" I nervously asked.

"There was quite a bit of damage to one area of her brain, which is where memories are stored. There is a great possibility that she won't remember anything."

"You mean she won't remember the accident, right?"

"That, and possibly her life. To be honest, I'd never seen this kind of damage before."

"You're telling me she won't remember who she is or anything about her life?"

"I'm saying it's a possibility," he spoke. "We won't know until she wakes up. I'm very sorry."

Two days had passed, and I hadn't left her side. Her grandmother flew in from Minnesota and sat in the chair next to Quinn's bed, placing her hand on hers.

A few hours later, I went down to the cafeteria to grab something to eat. I was gone an hour, and when I approached Quinn's room, her grandmother was standing outside her door while two doctors and a couple of nurses were in with her.

"What's going on?" I asked her grandmother.

She looked at me as tears streamed down her face and she placed her hand on my cheek.

"Quinn woke up and she has no memory of the last five years. She thought she was still twelve years old, and when I told her about the accident and her parents, she freaked out and they had to sedate her."

I swallowed the hard lump in my throat as my eyes swelled with tears.

"I'm so sorry, Noah."

I stood outside the window of her room and stared at her as she rested peacefully. She needed me, and she didn't even know it.

"Noah, the best thing you can do for her is to let her be. She doesn't know you and she has a long, difficult recovery ahead of her. I'm taking her back to Minnesota with me, and you're leaving for Yale in a couple of weeks."

"I can't go. I can't leave her. I won't leave her."

"The Quinn you knew is gone, Noah. She has been through so much and she's going to need to rebuild her life. She'll never get those five years back and it's going to be very hard on her. Do you want to add to that? I know what the two of you had was special, but in her mind, she still feels like a twelve-year-old girl. As much as you want to be her hero and save her from all of this, you can't. If you truly love Quinn, you'll let her go and you'll let her heal. She doesn't have any room in her life for you anymore. Things are different now and you need to leave her alone. If you don't, you'll only make things worse for her. You have your own life and future ahead of you. Don't compromise that over a girl who doesn't even know who you are."

"I love her." I furrowed my brows and cocked my head.

"I know you do, and that's why you have to do what's best for her. You're both so young and her life is completely changed and different now. The aftermath of this isn't going to be easy for her. Just walk away now and move on with your life. Here." She reached into her pocket.

"The nurse gave this to me. She was wearing it the night of the accident."

She placed the locket I had given her in my hand, and I gripped it tight as tears formed in my eyes.

⚅⚄

A WEEK HAD PASSED, AND I RESPECTED HER GRANDMOTHER'S WISHES and stayed away, until I couldn't any longer. I needed to be sure she didn't remember me. Maybe once she saw me, she would. I had this dream that I walked into her room and a bright smile crossed her face the moment she saw me because she remembered who I was and how much I loved her.

I stopped by the hospital with a bouquet of red roses and waited down the hallway until her grandmother left the room. Once she did, I slowly walked inside, and Quinn looked at me. My heart started to rapidly beat.

"Can I help you?" she asked.

"Oh, I'm sorry. I must have the wrong room," I spoke. "Isn't this 4323?"

"No. It's 4332."

"How dumb am I mixing up the room numbers like that." I smiled.

"It's okay. It's happens."

"Do you mind if I ask why you're in here?" I asked with caution. "You look a little banged up."

"I was in a car accident."

"I'm sorry." I gave her a sympathetic look.

"Thank you," she softly spoke.

"Here." I smiled as I handed her the flowers. "I want you to have these."

"No. That's okay. You bought them for the person you're visiting." She tried handing them back to me.

"Keep them. I can get more. Anyway, I'm sorry about your accident." I swallowed hard. "Let them brighten your day."

I turned around, and as I began to walk out of the room, I heard her voice.

"Thank you. That's very kind of you."

I slowly closed my eyes as I could feel the tears rise.

"You're welcome. I hope you feel better soon."

I walked out and left the love of my life behind. Tears streamed down my face as I walked down the long hallway to the elevator.

❧ 3 ❧

TWELVE YEARS LATER

Noah
      I moaned as I opened my eyes and felt the arm of last
      night's fuck draped around me. Glancing at the clock that
sat on the nightstand, I saw it was seven a.m. My head felt like
someone had taken a sledgehammer to it as I attempted to remember
the events of last night.

"Good morning," she spoke as her lips pressed firmly against
my back.

"Hey," I spoke as I removed her arm from me and climbed out
of bed.

"Where are you going?"

"I need to take a quick shower and get to work."

"Want some company?"

"No. That's okay. I'm in a hurry."

I stepped into the shower and let the hot water soothe my aching
head. Once I was finished, I put my clothes on from last night while
the girl lay in bed and watched me.

"I ordered room service. Can't you just stay and have breakfast?"
she asked.

"No. I have to go. Thanks for last night." I grabbed my wallet off the dresser. "I'll make sure the room is paid for."

"Am I ever going to see you again?"

I stopped with my hand on the door handle but didn't turn around to face her.

"No. Last night was a one-time thing."

I exited the hotel and walked the two blocks to the office. I needed the fresh air.

"Good morning, Noah," my personal assistant Ellen spoke.

"Morning," I mumbled as I went into my office and shut the door.

I always kept a closet full of suits when I didn't make it home the night before. After changing, I dabbed on some cologne to try and mask the smell of whiskey that still lingered on me.

"Ellen, I need coffee now," I spoke in a stern voice as I pressed the intercom button.

A few moments later, she stepped into my office and set the mug on my desk.

"Where are the last quarter reports?" I asked in a smug tone.

"They're sitting to the left of you," she replied. "Don't forget about the art gallery event tonight."

"Shit. Is that tonight?"

"Yes, and you're taking Claudia."

"Claudia?" I shook my head. "Which one is she again?"

"Long red hair, green eyes, about five foot seven. I take it you had another rough night."

"It was rough alright." I smirked. "Did you pick up my tux?"

"I did. It's hanging in your bedroom."

"Thanks. Do me a favor and get me two aspirin. I need it before I go in to speak to my father."

"Will do, Noah." A smug look crossed her face.

"Don't give me that look, Ellen."

"What look?" she asked with a raised brow as she walked out of my office.

I knew she didn't approve of my lifestyle. Ellen Debrow had known me since I was thirteen years old when she first started working at Kingston International as a personal assistant to my father. Once I graduated from Yale and took on the position of Chief Operating Officer, my father handed her down to me. I knew he did it so she could keep an eye on me.

The day I walked out of Quinn's hospital room, I became a changed man. A man whose world that was once filled with light and happiness suddenly went dark. A world filled with sex and booze just to numb the pain I'd felt inside. I once loved my life, and now, I just existed. I threw myself into my studies at Yale, which allowed me to get my MBA a year early. I didn't love anyone, and I couldn't bring myself to ever again. Women threw themselves at me all the time, but I never saw them as anything more than just sex, something I couldn't go without for more than three days just to feel something again. I was young, I was rich, and I was the prodigal son of Grant Kingston, which instantly threw me on the list of one of New York's most eligible bachelors, a title I had no interest in. I was bitter, arrogant, and for the most part, a total dick. But I didn't care, and no one was going to change me.

"Here is your aspirin," Ellen spoke as she walked into my office and handed them to me with a glass of water.

"Thanks. Is he in his office?"

"Yes, and he's asking if you're here."

I sighed as I got up from my chair, buttoned my dark gray suitcoat, and headed to his office.

"Morning, Dad," I spoke as I stepped inside.

"Morning, son. Have a seat." He looked up at me through his black-rimmed glasses. "I won't be able to make it tonight to the art gallery, but you'll be there, right?"

"Yeah, I'll be there. Why aren't you going?"

"I have to fly to Hong Kong. There's an issue with one of our contracts with the manufacturer."

"Is Mom going with you?"

"Actually, she is." He smiled. "We'll be gone for a couple of weeks, so I need you to look after things here."

"Yeah. Of course."

"You reek like booze, Noah."

"I went out last night."

"Your mother and I were talking, and we thought maybe this all would have passed by now. It's been twelve years, son. You're thirty years old now. Don't you think it's time to stop all this partying you're doing?"

"I know how long it's been, Dad. I don't party that much."

"All I'm saying is that we have a reputation to uphold here at Kingston International. I can't have the future CEO running around every night boozing it up and taking strange women home. You need to start thinking about settling down. You can't continue to live your life like this, son."

"Settling down will never be an option for me and you damn well know it."

"You need to go back into therapy, Noah."

"Therapy?" I laughed. "What a joke. There's no amount of therapy in the world that can fix me. It didn't before, and it certainly won't now."

"Then maybe you need to turn to God for help."

That was the worst thing my father could have ever said to me.

"God?" I spoke through gritted teeth. "The same God who took the love of my life's memory away? The same God who killed her parents? No thanks. As far as I'm concerned, there is no God, only the devil himself. If you'll excuse me, I have work I need to do."

I got up from my seat and stormed out of his office.

﹩ 4 ﹩

Q*uinn*
      I finally got the last of my boxes unpacked in my
new apartment, located in the heart of Soho. I smiled as
I looked around the eleven-hundred-square-foot, two-bedroom, one-
bath place that was now my new home. I had already been here a week
and was loving it.

Since the accident, my grandmother moved me to Minnesota,
where she took care of me while I healed and tried to accept losing five
years of my life and my parents. It took a long time. I went into a
severe depression, where I needed to be hospitalized at one point for
over a month. That was where I met Dr. Brandon Cooper, a therapist
who seemed to be the only person who could help me move on with
my life. He was tough and a bit rough around the edges, but he got
through to me when no one else could. I got my shit together, studied,
and got my GED at the age of twenty. For my eighteenth birthday, my
grandmother bought me a new camera, which sat in the box up on the
closet shelf for two years. The one thing I remembered was I showed
an interest in photography when I was twelve years old, but I didn't
remember it becoming a passion of mine. It was after I got my GED
when I took the camera out of the box for the first time, and even

though I didn't remember how much I loved it, I felt it as I held it in my hands.

I discovered I had a natural talent and captured things in different ways than other photographers. I took a few classes at the local community college and learned what I could. But for me, photography couldn't be taught. It was just an instinct I was born with.

I went on a month-long road trip, or what I liked to call a soul-searching trip, by myself and traveled through a few different states, taking pictures of the mountains, lakes, animals, and some historic landmarks. My grandmother was scared out of her mind for me because she felt I was too young to go alone, but it was something I had to do. And I was happy I did. I blogged my entire trip and posted all of the pictures I took. When I returned home, I received a call from *Time Magazine* asking if they could purchase a few of my pictures to publish in their upcoming edition. I proudly accepted their generous offer, which in turn led to other companies using me as a freelance photographer, which had become my career the past nine years. It was a career that paid good money. In addition to doing free-lance, I set up a website and a shop selling my photographs to anyone who was interested. About a month ago, I received a call from an art gallery in New York that stumbled upon my website and was intrigued by my work. They wanted to commission me to display and sell my work in their gallery. This was a huge opportunity for me and I knew it was one I couldn't refuse. This was my chance. When I told my grand-mother about it, a strange look crossed her face. She didn't want me to move back there and I couldn't understand why.

"Grandma, I don't understand why you have such a problem with me moving to New York."

"Because, Quinn, that place is filled with a gap in your life. I brought you here to escape that and to help you heal. Now you want to throw all that away and move back to the place that you don't even remember since you were twelve years old."

"Dr. Cooper thinks it's a good idea."

"I don't care what Dr. Cooper thinks. I need you here with me."

"Well, I'm sorry you feel that way, but I have to live my own life. I am so grateful for everything you have done for me over the years, but it's time you let me go."

I walked down the street to Starbucks to grab a coffee before I went dress shopping. Tonight was the night that the art gallery was hosting a special event for only elite guests. And since my work was on display, they asked me if I could be there. The week I had been here, I'd look around at the thousands of people walking down the street and wondered if I knew anyone or if anyone would recognize me. I wanted to know more about the five years I lost. I needed to know. The only thing my grandmother told me was that I loved photography and I was a good student. I had asked her if I was dating anyone prior to the accident and she told me that I wasn't interested in boys because I was too focused on school and my hobby. I dated on and off back in Minnesota but never met anyone that I could care enough about to stay with. I tried. I really did. I even dated James for eight months. My longest relationship ever. He was sweet and kind, but I just didn't have the same feelings he had for me. He talked about marriage and how I was the one. It freaked me out because I didn't see myself with him or with any guy I'd dated. My love life was like a revolving door; one would leave, and another would enter, but only for short periods of time. I was beginning to wonder if there was something wrong with me.

I found the perfect black dress at Saks on the clearance rack, and with the money I saved, I decided to treat myself to a new pair of black heels. After I arrived home, I took a shower, applied my makeup, put some beachy waves in my long brown hair, and slipped into my dress. I was starting to get nervous. This was my first display in an art gallery, and I wasn't sure what to expect. What if people hated my photos? I sighed as I grabbed my purse and took a cab to the gallery.

꧁ 5 ꧂

*N**oah**

"Ellen, call Claudia for me and tell her that there was a change of plans and I won't be taking her to the art gallery tonight."

"Why not?" She cocked her head at me.

"Because I don't feel like dealing with her or any woman tonight."

"Is that what you want me to tell her?"

"No. Of course not. Just make something up."

"Noah," she sighed.

"Just do it, Ellen."

I walked into my office and shut the door. Walking over to my bar, I poured a shot of whiskey and threw it down the back of my throat. Pulling my phone from my pocket, I called my best friend, Henry.

"Hey, Noah."

"Henry, what are you doing tonight?"

"Don't have any plans as of now. Why?"

"Kingston is sponsoring this art gallery event tonight and I want you to come with me."

"You're not taking one of your many women with you?"

"Nah. Not tonight. There will be free food and booze. Not to mention hot chicks in skimpy dresses with their tits hanging out and their pussies free of panties."

"Count me in, bro. What time?"

"Meet me at my house at seven. I'll have a car waiting to take us. Oh, and by the way, it's black tie."

"Awesome. Can't wait. See you later."

Henry Kilpatrick was my roommate at Yale. At first, I was a complete dick to him. But he was a good guy and he helped me through some really shitty days, even though I didn't deserve it. He was the only person I ever told about Quinn and he'd stuck by me ever since. After we both graduated a year early and in the top five percent of our class, I took my position at my father's company and he landed a job as a stockbroker on Wall Street.

I left the office and went home for a quick shower and to change into my tux. After I was done getting dressed, I poured myself a whiskey and took it out on the balcony, where I stared out at the city lights. The emptiness I felt reinforced itself inside me and the last place I wanted to go tonight was that damn art gallery. I'd much rather stay in and drink myself to sleep.

The doorbell rang and startled me from deep thoughts.

"Hey, you ready to go?" Henry asked.

"Yeah. I guess." I sighed.

"What's wrong?"

"Nothing. Just a long day," I replied as I shut and locked the door.

We arrived at the art gallery where many of Manhattan's elite began to fill the space.

"Noah," Charles Caprese spoke as he placed his hand on my shoulder. "It's good to see you again."

"Charles." I nodded. "How have you been?"

"No complaints on my end. "Where's your father?"

"He had to fly out to Hong Kong this evening for a business matter."

"That son of a bitch." He smiled. "Always finding a way to get out of these things."

The waiter walked by with a tray of champagne and I quickly grabbed one. After leaving Charles, I looked around for Henry, who was busy talking to a couple about stocks. I walked around the gallery and looked at the paintings that hung on the wall until I made it to the photograph section. The pictures were stunning, and for some reason, I seemed to be captivated by them.

"Mr. Kingston, welcome," Kara, the manager of the art gallery spoke.

"Thank you, Kara. Is this a new collection? I don't recall seeing these here before."

"Yes." She smiled with excitement. "Aren't they lovely?"

"They are. May I ask who the photographer is?"

"Her name is Quinn Stevens."

Suddenly, I could feel the air in my lungs diminish as my heart started racing.

"Oh, there she is. Quinn, can you come over here, please?" Kara spoke.

I slowly turned around as my eyes fixated on her. My god, she was so beautiful.

"Quinn, I would like you to meet Noah Kingston. His family is the one who sponsored this event. Mr. Kingston, this is Quinn Stevens, the artist responsible for these lovely photos."

"It's nice to meet you, Mr. Kingston." Quinn smiled as she extended her hand.

I swallowed hard as I slowly placed my hand in hers.

"It's nice to meet you as well, Quinn."

My heart felt like it was trying to escape my chest as a wave of shock overtook my body.

"Mr. Kingston was just admiring your work," Kara said.

"Really?" she asked with a smile. The same smile that lit up my life since the first day I'd met her.

"Yes. Your photographs are excellent."

"Thank you. I appreciate it." Her smile grew wide.

"Hey, Noah?" I heard Henry's voice from behind.

"If you'll excuse me for a moment," I spoke as I stared into Quinn's eyes before walking away.

"Who was that?" Henry asked.

I placed my hand on his shoulder for a moment and then headed towards the door of the gallery.

"Noah, wait. Where are you going?"

I stepped outside and let the brisk, cool air fill my lungs as I stood there against the building, lowered my head, and slowly closed my eyes to try and calm the fuck down.

"What the hell is the matter with you?" Henry asked. "Are you feeling okay?"

I looked up and stared at him for a moment before speaking.

"She's here, Henry."

"Who's here? Dude, I've never seen you like this before."

"Quinn. Quinn is here. I just spoke with her." I ran my hand down my face.

"What? What is she doing here? Did she recognize you?"

"Her photographs are on display in the gallery, and no, she didn't recognize me. Fuck!" I ran my hands through my hair.

"Noah, calm down," he spoke as he placed his hand on my shoulder. "Just calm down. This is a good thing. You thought you'd never see her again. Is she married?"

"I didn't see a ring on her finger."

"Okay, good. That's a good start. Shit, bro. I can't believe this."

"*You* can't believe this? I need to go back in there and talk to her. I need to find out what her life has been like since the accident, what she's been doing and if she's seeing anyone."

"First of all, you need to stop and think for a minute, because you sound like a stalker. You just can't go up to her and start bombarding her with questions. You're going to scare her off."

"I guess you're right. Jesus, Henry, my head is so fucked up right now."

"Then un-fuck it up, calm down, and casually walk up to her and start a conversation. You're a complete stranger to her. Don't forget that."

"You're right. Thanks." I gave him a small smile.

I took in a deep breath and went back inside the gallery to look for her.

6

Q*uinn*

    I looked around the gallery, scanning the crowd to see if I could see him. The first thing I noticed about him were his blue eyes. They weren't ordinary blue eyes; they were bright and striking. He stood about six feet two with dark brown hair that was styled in a mid-taper cut and a perfectly kept five o'clock shadow that accented his masculine jawline. He was incredibly sexy, and the moment our hands touched, I felt something tear through my body that I'd never in my life felt before. It was almost as if life had been breathed into me. I knew that sounded stupid and if I were to tell anyone that, they'd think I was crazy. I almost felt crazy just for thinking it.

"Hello again," I heard his smoky voice from behind.

I turned around, and instantly, a smile found its way across my lips.

"Hi."

"I'm sorry about earlier. My friend Henry needed to speak with me. Anyway, I'm interested in buying one of your photographs. Actually, all of them." He smiled.

"Really? All of them?" I let out a light laugh.

"Yes. I think they're perfect for display throughout our department store."

"Wow. Okay." I bit down on my bottom lip as I could feel my cheeks blush. "All you have to do is let Kara know."

"I definitely will." The corners of his mouth curved upwards. "Do you live here in New York?"

"I just moved here a week ago. I'm originally from Minnesota. Well, actually, I lived here for seventeen years and then I moved to Minnesota, and now I feel like I'm back where I belong."

"Any specific reason you moved out to Minnesota?"

"It's a long and complicated story."

"Hello, Noah." A tall, lanky woman with long, blonde, straight hair smiled as she placed her hand on his chest.

"Amelia, I didn't know you were going to be here," he spoke.

"You would have if you would've called me like you promised you would. I'm sorry to interrupt, but there's someone I'd like you to meet."

"I'm in the middle of a conversation, Amelia. Whoever you want me to meet can wait."

"No, darling." She hooked her arm around his. "I want you to meet him now before he leaves."

She began to lead him away and he turned his head and looked at me.

"I'm sorry," he mouthed.

I gave him a small smile and grabbed a glass of champagne.

"He's one sexy man, isn't he?" Kara asked with a smile as she stood next to me.

"He definitely is, and he's buying every single one of my photographs."

"That's wonderful, Quinn. Congratulations."

"Thanks." I grinned. "He said they will be going on display in different areas of Kingston's Department Store."

"He likes you. He keeps stealing small glances from across the gallery."

"You think so?"

"I do. He has quite a reputation, though. He loves his whiskey and he sees a lot of different women. He's untamable. I know you just moved here, and I want you to be careful where he's concerned. He's a sexy bad boy."

"Thanks for the heads up." I brought my glass up to my lips.

Noah couldn't seem to get away from the people who kept him busy in deep conversations. I went into Kara's office and grabbed my camera. She had asked me if I could take some pictures of the event. So I walked around and did just that, taking an extra few of Noah from a distance. It was getting late and I was tired, so I decided to call it a night and go home. After stepping through the door of my apartment, I kicked off my shoes, took off my makeup, changed into my pajamas, climbed into bed with my laptop, and downloaded all the pictures I had taken. Noah Kingston was just as sexy in pictures as he was in person. Something felt weird the moment I saw him. He seemed familiar to me in some way. I felt as if we had met before, but I knew that wasn't possible.

I lay in bed and thought about what Kara had told me about him, yet, when I looked into his eyes, I didn't see the person she described. Maybe I was just lust struck.

7

Noah

I tried to get away from everyone and anyone who held me hostage in business conversations. By the time I was able to sneak away, I looked all over the gallery for Quinn.

"Kara, do you know where Quinn is?"

"She left already."

"Damn it," I spoke with disappointment. "Do you know why she left?"

"She said since her photographs sold, there was no need for her to stick around. Plus, she was tired."

"Thanks, Kara." I placed my hand on her arm. "By the way, good job with the event."

"Thank you, Mr. Kingston." She smiled.

I walked away with a sick feeling in my stomach.

"Noah, how about we go back to my place for a nightcap?" Amelia seductively asked as she ran her finger down my arm.

"Not tonight, Amelia. I have other plans," I spoke as I walked away. I found Henry and asked him if he was ready to leave.

As soon as I got home, I poured myself a whiskey and stared out at the brightly lit city as I threw the liquid down the back of my throat.

Quinn moved back here, and I still couldn't believe it. I thought she was beautiful when I first met her all those years ago, but now, she was even more beautiful as a twenty-nine-year-old woman. Indecision stirred inside me about this whole situation. I felt like I needed to tell her about me, who I really was, and everything we shared twelve years ago. But then, what if she hated me for leaving her after the accident instead of sticking around and explaining to her that she was the love of my life and we had our entire future planned out. Just knowing she was in the same city and not being able to have her in my bed was killing me.

᪥

THE NEXT MORNING, I STUMBLED OUT OF BED, HUNGOVER BETWEEN the champagne at the art gallery and the whiskey I drank when I got home.

"You're late," Ellen spoke as she followed me into my office.

"I know," I harshly spoke.

"Who kept you in bed this morning?" she asked.

"Nobody."

"You know, with your father being gone, you need to make sure you're here on time."

"Damn it, Ellen!" I shouted. "I know that."

"What happened last night at the art gallery?" she asked as she took the seat across from my desk. "And don't tell me 'nothing,' because the way you're acting right now is telling me different."

I sat there, leaned back in my chair, wondering if I should tell her about Quinn. She knew her, and she knew what we had.

"I saw Quinn last night," I sighed.

"Quinn Stevens?" she asked in shock as she cocked her head at me.

"Yes. She was at the art gallery. She had some photographs on display there."

"Did you talk to her?"

"Of course I did, and I bought all her pictures."

"There was no change, was there? She still doesn't remember you?"

"No. I was a complete stranger in her eyes. God, Ellen, you should see her. She's so beautiful. She lives here now. She moved to New York about a week ago."

"Noah, that's wonderful news! The two of you can have a second chance."

"It's not that simple, Ellen. What if she doesn't like me or isn't interested?"

"You won't know unless you try. She fell for you once before."

"She was sixteen then. People change."

"You still love her, and that never changed for you. But you need to clean up your act, Noah."

I let out a long sigh.

"Anyway, you have a meeting at ten o'clock with Ken Bartlett in conference room three," she spoke.

"Can I get some coffee and a couple of aspirin?"

"Sure. I'll bring them right in." She smiled as she walked out of my office.

I turned my chair around and stared out at the busy city. Traffic lined the streets and the hustle and bustle of people rushing from point A to B filled the sidewalks. I needed to see Quinn again. It wasn't an option.

"Here's your coffee and aspirin," Ellen spoke as she walked into my office.

"Thanks. I want you to get a team together, head over to the gallery, and collect the photos I purchased from Quinn. Then I want you to take them over to Kingston and have them put up immediately. I want them up by this afternoon. Everyone is to drop what they're doing to make it happen. Understand?"

"Yes, Noah."

"Let me know when it's done."

⚜

By the time I finished my meeting, it was noon. As I was walking back to my office, my phone rang. It was Ellen.

"Is it done?"

"They're finishing it up now."

"Good. I want you to call the gallery and get Quinn's phone number. Call her and tell her to meet you at Kingston's Department Store. Call me back and let me know what she says."

"What if she's busy and she can't?"

"Then set up a time for today when she's available. Don't fail me, Ellen. I'm counting on you. And another thing, do not let on that you know her."

"I won't. I'll call you back."

I sat down behind my desk and took in a deep breath. A few moments later, my phone rang.

"What did she say?" I asked as I answered.

"She will be here in thirty minutes," Ellen spoke.

"Okay." A smile fell across my lips. "I'll be there soon."

❧ 8 ❧

Q*uinn*

I was in line at Starbucks when I received Ellen's call and I couldn't have been more thrilled. After grabbing my coffee from the counter, I hailed a cab to Kingston's Department Store where I was supposed to meet Ellen on the first floor by the doors. When I walked in, a woman in her fifties with blonde shoulder-length hair and brown eyes looked directly at me but didn't say a word.

"Ellen?" I asked as she stared at me.

"Yes. You must be Quinn Stevens. It's wonderful to meet you." She smiled as she extended her hand.

"It's nice to meet you too. Thank you for inviting me here."

"You're welcome. I'm happy you were available. Come with me."

She led me to the escalator, and we rode it up to the second floor.

"So you work with Mr. Kingston?" I asked.

"Yes, I'm Noah's personal assistant. I was quite surprised when he told me he bought all of your photographs, but then after seeing them, I can understand why. You're very talented."

"Thank you." I graciously smiled.

We reached the second floor, and from across the store, I saw

Noah standing in front of one of my photographs that was displayed on the wall.

"Noah, what are you doing here?" Ellen asked. "I thought you were in a meeting."

"I was, but it ended earlier than I thought it would, so I decided to come here and make sure the photographs were displayed properly. Hello, Quinn." He smiled.

"Hello, Mr. Kingston." I smiled back.

"You can call me Noah."

I could feel the heat rise in my cheeks.

"Ellen, I need you to call Lawrence Canfield and tell him I need the product contracts by tomorrow afternoon."

"Of course, Noah. I'll go call him now."

"Let me ask you," I smiled, "does the Chief Operating Officer of a company always come to see if things are displayed properly?"

"Sometimes, yes." He grinned. "Now let me ask you something. Will you join me for dinner tonight?"

"You want to take me to dinner?" I asked as my belly fluttered.

"Yes, I do. If you don't want to, I understand. I mean, I know you just moved here and probably don't know many people."

"No. I don't know a lot of people and I would love to have dinner with you."

"Excellent." The corners of his mouth curved upwards. "I can pick you up around seven. Is that fine?"

"Seven is perfect. I can text you my address." I pulled my phone from my purse.

He rattled off his phone number and I entered it into my phone. Then I sent him my address.

"I'll see you at seven, Quinn Stevens."

"I'll be ready." I bashfully smiled.

Noah

I WALKED OUT OF MY STORE WITH A HUGE GRIN ACROSS MY FACE. I'D been dreaming of this moment for the past twelve years. I pulled my phone from my pocket and dialed Carbone.

"Carbone, this is Helen, how may I help you?"

"Helen, it's Noah Kingston. I need a quiet corner table for two for seven thirty."

"Very good, Mr. Kingston. You're all set for seven thirty."

"Thank you."

I ended the call and climbed into the back of my Escalade.

"How did it go?" Sean asked.

"I'm taking her to dinner tonight." I smiled.

"Noah, that's great news."

"Do me a favor and don't mention any of this to my parents. I don't want them knowing until I'm ready."

"I won't. You know you can trust me."

Nervousness settled inside me the more I thought about tonight. I needed to be very careful with what I'd say to her and I needed to remember not to bombard her with questions, even though I had a million of them for her. When I arrived back to work, Ellen followed me into my office.

"She's just as lovely now as she was twelve years ago." She smiled.

"She definitely is," I spoke as I sat down at my desk. "I'm taking her to dinner tonight."

"Where are you taking her?" she asked.

"Carbone." I smiled. "It's where I took her on our first date. She always loved Italian food."

"Noah," Ellen spoke as she walked closer to my desk. "I hope you're not expecting her to remember anything by taking her there."

"I'm not. I know she doesn't remember."

Ellen gave me a small smile before walking out of my office. I leaned back in my chair, placed my hands behind my head, and thought about Quinn. I couldn't wait to see her tonight.

꽃 9 꽃

Q*uinn*

       I made myself a cup of coffee, sat down on the couch, and Skyped Dr. Cooper.

"Hello, Quinn." He smiled. "How's New York?"

"Hi, Dr. Cooper. New York is really good. It feels right being back here. I need to talk to you about something."

"Okay. What's on your mind?" he asked as he folded his hands.

"I met someone, a man, and I can't explain this feeling I have inside me."

"What kind of feeling do you have?"

"A feeling I've never felt before with anyone. I mean, I know we just met, but I feel like I've known him my whole life. There's something about him that feels like home. Ugh, Dr. Cooper, am I crazy? Because I feel really crazy right now."

He gave me a small smile. "No, Quinn, you're not crazy. Something inside you recognized him before your mind could even comprehend it. It happens. There are times when we feel a strong connection with someone that we can't explain. I know you're looking for an explanation, but there isn't one. So my advice to you is to enjoy yourself, get to know him, and forget about wanting to know why."

"Thanks, Dr. Cooper. I'll do just that. He's taking me to dinner tonight and I can't wait to see him."

"Have fun, and remember, don't question things. You've been doing that since the first day you walked into my office. Have you spoken to your grandmother?"

"I called her when I first got here. I can tell she isn't happy about my move, and I do feel bad for that. She's really done so much for me since the accident."

"I know she has and it's natural to feel bad, but this is your life and you need to do what's best for you. You can't worry about what everyone else wants you to do. They aren't living your life."

"Thanks, Dr. Cooper." I smiled. "I need to go get ready for my date."

"Have fun and let me know how it goes."

"I will."

I signed off and went into the bathroom to take a shower. As the warm water streamed down my body, I couldn't stop thinking about Noah and what I said to Dr. Cooper about how he felt like home. Was that even possible to feel that way about someone you didn't even know? I needed to stop thinking about it and take Dr. Cooper's advice.

Just as I slipped on my heels, I heard my intercom ring, so I pushed the button to open the door and nervously waited for Noah to come up.

"Hi." He smiled as he handed me a bouquet of white roses. "These are for you."

"Thank you." I grinned as I brought them up to my nose and took in their lovely fragrance. "Come in."

He walked inside and shut the door while I went to the kitchen and pulled a vase from the cabinet.

"You have a really nice place here, and by the way, you look incredible."

"Thank you and thank you." A shy smile crossed my lips as I filled the vase with water.

After arranging the flowers, I set them on my dining room table.

"I think that's the perfect spot for them," I spoke.

"They look great there. Are you ready? Our reservation is for seven thirty."

"Yes." I grabbed my purse and we headed out the door.

My pheromones were at an all-time high just by his scent—a scent that seemed familiar to me, but I couldn't figure out where I knew it from. None of the other guys I dated smelled like he did. He smelled earthy, like sandalwood. It was a scent I found myself highly attracted to. We walked out of my building and he helped me into the back of his Escalade.

"Sean, I'd like you to meet Quinn Stevens. Quinn, this is my driver, Sean."

"It's nice to meet you, Miss Stevens." He smiled.

"It's nice to meet you too, Sean."

"Have you ever eaten here?" Noah asked as we arrived at Carbone.

"I think I'd eaten here with my parents when I was a child," I replied.

Suddenly, my nerves started to get the best of me at the thought about telling him of my past and how I lost five years of my life. He was going to ask questions and I'd eventually have to tell him.

When we walked into the restaurant, the hostess led us to a quiet table in the corner.

"Do you drink wine?" Noah asked me.

"I do." I smiled.

"We'll have a bottle of your finest wine," Noah spoke to the waitress that was standing at our table.

"Very good, Mr. Kingston. I'll bring that right over."

I picked up the menu and looked it over.

"Everything sounds so good. I'm not sure what to get," I spoke.

"May I make a suggestion?"

"Of course."

"I would start with the wedding soup and the lobster ravioli. I think you'll like it."

"Both sound delicious." I smiled. "I think I'll order that."

The waitress came back to our table, poured us each a glass of wine, and then set the bottle down on the table.

"Are you two ready to order?"

34

"We will both have the wedding soup and lobster ravioli," Noah spoke.

"Excellent choices. I'll go put that in for you."

As soon as she walked away, Noah picked up his glass and held it up to me.

"Welcome to New York City and to selling all of your photographs in one night." He grinned.

"Thank you." The corners of my mouth curved upwards. "Thank you for buying all of them." I lightly tapped my glass against his.

"I knew they'd look great in the store." He winked.

"So, tell me about Noah Kingston." I took a sip of my wine.

"Well, I was born and raised here in New York. After I graduated from high school, I attended Yale University and then went to work at Kingston International headquarters as my father's right-hand man. Your turn." He picked up his glass.

"My life is a little more complicated," I spoke.

"Let me ask you this. You told me that you used to live in New York for the first seventeen years of your life, then you moved to Minnesota. What made you decide to move back here?"

"Well," the nervous fluttering in my belly intensified, "my grandmother moved me away and to her home in Minnesota after my parents and I were in a car accident. Both my parents died."

❧ 10 ❧

Noah

After she spoke those words, I felt like I was reliving that moment back in the hospital the night of the accident. Pain grew in my heart as I relived the flashbacks of the doctor telling me she was in surgery and her parents didn't make it.

"Quinn, I'm sorry."

"Thanks." She placed her napkin on her lap as the waitress set down our food in front of us.

"So your grandmother just uprooted you? I mean, you were probably in your last year of high school then."

"Yeah. Minnesota is her home and she needed to take care of me. She was the only family I had, except for a few cousins in Florida."

I sat there and wondered if she was going to tell me about losing five years of her life or if it would be too difficult for her.

"I was seriously injured in the car accident and I suffered a severe brain injury. When I woke up, I had discovered that I lost the last five years of my life. I was seventeen at the time, but I still believed I was twelve. Five years of my life prior to the accident were completely wiped out from my memory."

"I don't know what to say except I'm sorry that happened to you. It must have been very difficult to accept."

"It was. I went into a severe depression and—"

"And what?" I asked as fear swept over me.

"I can't believe I'm telling you this. I've never told anyone before," she spoke with hesitation.

I reached across the table and took hold of her hand.

"It's okay. You can tell me anything."

She took in a deep breath. "I took a bottle of sleeping pills. God, you must think I'm crazy."

I could see the tears swell in her eyes as my heart broke.

"No. I don't think you're crazy at all. That had to be most terrifying thing anyone could ever go through."

"I just couldn't deal with the constant trying to remember and I just wanted to end it. But my grandmother found me, called 911, and I spent a month in a psychiatric hospital."

All I wanted to do was reach over, grab her, and hold her tightly in my arms. Maybe if I would have stuck around, she wouldn't have attempted to take her life. Guilt started to rise inside me.

"I'm so sorry," I spoke.

"Don't be, because that was the best thing that ever could have happened to me. I met this wonderful doctor. His name is Dr. Brandon Cooper and he was the only one who could get through to me and help me see that it didn't matter that I couldn't remember five years of my life. All that mattered was that I was creating new memories and moving forward. After I got out of the hospital, I continued to see him three times a week, then two times a week, and eventually, one time a week. I discovered I loved photography and that I was good at it. So that's what I focused on. I went on a soul-searching trip, per Dr. Cooper, and it really helped. I took tons of pictures of the places I was at and *Time Magazine* called me up and wanted to purchase a few for their upcoming edition. After that, my career as a photographer took off and now I do a bunch of freelance work for different companies and people."

"How did you get with the art gallery?" I asked.

"They saw my photographs online and told me they were interested in commissioning me for them to sell in their gallery. So I accepted and moved back here."

"What about your grandmother? How did she feel about you moving back here?"

"She was upset about it and tried to talk me out of it, but I didn't let her. There was this huge part of me that knew this is where I belonged, and it was time. For some reason, and one that I can't explain, I had this strong sense that I needed to come back here."

"Well, I'm happy you decided to move back." I smiled.

We finished dinner and then took a walk through Greenwich Village. The night air was getting colder as October settled upon us. I wanted desperately to hold her hand, so I lightly touched her fingers as we walked side by side. And before I knew it, our hands were entwined. I wanted this moment to last forever.

"Are you cold?" I asked her.

"A little bit. I didn't think it would get this cold already."

I took off my suitcoat and wrapped it around her shoulders, keeping my arm around her the entire time to keep her warm. She looked up at me with a smile and all I could think about was kissing her beautiful lips again. I wasn't sure how late we'd be out, so I sent Sean home for the night, and hailed us a cab back to her place. I walked her up to her apartment and she slid the key in the lock and opened the door.

"Thank you for dinner. I had a really good time." She smiled.

"You're welcome. Thank you for joining me. I had a really great time too."

I placed my hand on her cheek and softly stroked it as I stared down at her lips. I didn't want to push it and I didn't want her to think I only wanted sex, because I didn't. I mean, I did, but I'd wait for however long it took her to be ready if she wanted to. She reached up and surprised me as her lips brushed against mine. I felt as if I'd lost my breath. Our lips stayed locked together as the heat between us rose and so did my cock.

"Would you like to come in?" she asked.

"I'd love to."

❧ 11 ❧

Quinn

I'd never thrown myself at a man before and I certainly never had sex on a first date. I always waited at least until date five or six. But I couldn't help myself with Noah. I wanted him and a part of me felt like I needed him in ways I couldn't explain.

Our lips met again the minute we walked through the door as my fingers began to unbutton his shirt. He reached back and unzipped my dress, pushing it down from my shoulders as it fell to the ground. He broke our kiss as his eyes grazed over me from head to toe.

"You are so beautiful, Quinn," he whispered as his mouth traveled to my neck.

He picked me up, carried me into the bedroom, and gently laid me on the bed. I lay there in nothing but my bra and panties, staring at him while he removed his clothes. He reached in his wallet, took out a condom, and set it on my nightstand. He took down his underwear and I gasped at the well-endowed package that God graced him with. I smiled as I looked up at him and his muscular body hovered over mine. Our lips touched as his fingers traveled down my torso and down the front of my panties. Excitement shot through me as he dipped his finger inside. I arched my back and threw back my head as he explored me.

"You're so wet. Oh my god, you have me so turned on," he moaned.

He removed his finger and took down my panties, tossing them off the bed. My body grew in anticipation as his tongue traveled all the way down to my aroused and sensitive area. I was soaked with pleasure as he did things to me with his mouth that I'd never experienced before. I gripped the sides of my comforter as my body tightened and the most engaging orgasm I'd ever had ripped through me, leaving me out of breath and speechless. I brought my hands on each side of his head and guided him back up to me. His lips brushed against mine as he reached behind me and unhooked my bra. He stared at my naked breasts before taking my hardened peaks lightly between his teeth. As much as I loved the foreplay, I was desperate to feel him inside me.

He reached over to the nightstand and grabbed the condom. Ripping open the package, he took the condom out and rolled it over his hard cock. A smile fell upon my lips as he hovered over me and gently pushed himself inside.

Noah

SHE GREETED MY COCK WITH WARMTH AS SHE TOOK ME IN INCH BY inch until I was buried inside her. I never thought I'd make love to her again, but here I was, deep inside her just like when we were teenagers. The feeling was euphoric as I thrusted slowly in and out of her, staring into her baby blue eyes as her hands tangled through my hair. Another orgasm erupted from her and I wanted to hold out as long as I could because I didn't want this to end. I thrust in and out of her while my lips met hers and my hand held her wrists above her head. I picked up the pace as we both moaned in harmony and I finally exploded, straining out every last drop I could. I gently lowered myself on her as her arms around my neck tightened. She felt something. I know she did. I pulled out of her, kissed her lips with a smile, and removed the condom.

"It's pretty late. Maybe you should stay the night," she softly spoke.

"I would love to stay the night with you."

I climbed under the covers and held out my arm as she snuggled against me and her head found its place upon my chest.

"I don't want you to think I normally do this on first dates, because I don't."

"I don't think that." I kissed the top of her head.

"Can I tell you something without you thinking I'm crazy?" she asked.

"You can tell me anything and I would never think that."

Her fingers softly stroked my chest. "From the first moment I met you, you seemed so familiar to me."

I swallowed hard, trying to push down the lump that formed in my throat.

"People have told me that I have one of those familiar faces."

"Yeah. Maybe you do." She smiled as she lifted her head and looked at me.

"Did you have anyone special back in Minnesota?" I cautiously asked and being fully aware that I didn't want to know.

"I dated on and off, relationships usually lasted about a month or two. But my last one lasted about eight months. That was a record for me."

I wanted to tell her that we were together for over a year and that *I* was her record, but I couldn't.

"Eight months is a pretty good amount of time," I spoke as my heart ached, knowing she had been a part of someone else's life.

"I wasn't happy, and I felt bad for leading him to believe he meant more to me than he did. How about you?"

I closed my eyes for a moment as I carefully thought before I spoke.

"I was in a relationship once back when I was a teenager. It was the one and only relationship I'd ever had."

"Why?"

"Things happened, and I could no longer be a part of her life, so I went off to college and never looked back."

"Did she break your heart?" she asked in a soft voice.

"She didn't. The circumstances did. After that, I never wanted to be in a relationship again."

"I'm sorry," she said as I felt her lips press against my chest.

I tightened my grip around her as I inhaled a sharp breath.

"We should get some sleep," I spoke as I kissed the top of her head.

"Good night, Noah."

"Good night, Quinn."

❧ 12 ❧

Q*uinn*

I smiled as I felt Noah's arm wrapped tightly against me. Opening my eyes, I rolled over and watched him as he slept. I couldn't stop thinking about what he said to me last night about the one relationship he'd had. It was obvious that destroyed him and I suspected that was the reason for him being a "player," according to Kara.

He opened his sleepy eyes, and when he saw me staring at him, a smile graced his face.

"Good morning," he spoke.

"Good morning. How about some coffee?"

"I'd love some. What time is it?"

"Nine o'clock."

"Damn. I can't remember the last time I slept this late."

I softly brushed my lips against his before climbing out of bed. He grabbed hold of my wrist and pulled me back to him, rolling me on my back and hovering over me.

"I think coffee can wait." He smirked.

"You do?" I laughed.

"Yeah, I do."

After we made love, I put on my robe and headed to the kitchen. My head was spinning with delight and I couldn't recall a time when I was this happy. I popped a k-cup in the Keurig and made Noah's coffee first. As I was standing there waiting for it to finish, I felt his arms wrap around me from behind.

"Seeing it's Saturday, I have the day off, so I thought we could spend it together. Unless you have plans already."

"Nope. No plans, and I would love to spend the day together. Did you have anything in mind?" I asked as I handed him his coffee.

"I have a lot in mind that involves staying in bed all day and holding you in my arms."

"I like that idea." I bit down on my bottom lip.

"Yeah." He smiled as his lips brushed against mine.

"Yeah." I laughed.

"I was thinking we could head to Montauk. It's beautiful this time of year and my parents have a house there. We could spend the night and head back tomorrow."

"I'd like that. I've never been to Montauk."

"Okay. Grab a cup of coffee and pack an overnight bag. I'll make some calls." He kissed my lips.

I took my coffee into the bedroom and began packing a small bag. I'd never been to Montauk and I was excited to see it. But I was more excited to spend the whole weekend with him. This wasn't like me. I didn't do things like this with guys I'd just met, but he was different and I felt safe with him.

"We're all set. The helicopter will be ready in an hour."

"Helicopter?" I cocked my head.

"Yeah. The drive is three hours and we can be there by helicopter in thirty minutes. Are you afraid to fly?"

"No. I just have never been on a helicopter before."

"You'll love it. I promise." He walked over to me and gave me a kiss. "Are you almost ready? We have to stop by my place first."

"Yeah. Just let me grab a couple more things."

I zipped up my bag and Noah grabbed it off the bed and carried it for me. We climbed into the back of his Escalade where Sean was waiting for us by the curb. Once we reached his building, he grabbed hold of my hand and brought it up to his lips.

"I'll only be five minutes. I really want you to see my place, but it'll have to wait for when we have more time, so I can give you the grand tour." He smiled.

"Okay," I spoke.

Five minutes later, he was back like promised and we headed to where the helicopter was waiting for us. When we reached the helipad, a nervousness settled inside me.

"You'll be fine, Quinn. I promise," he spoke as he helped me up.

I held his hand the whole way there and with a tight grip. Once we landed, I let out a sigh of relief, even though it wasn't that bad.

"Where are we?" I asked as I stared ahead at the mansion in front of me.

"This is the Montauk family estate," he said.

"Wow."

"Wait until you see the inside."

We walked through the door and I felt like I had just stepped into a palace. The décor was meticulous as well as the wood trim and the two winding staircases that led to the second and third floors.

We spent the rest of the day shopping, eating, and seeing the beautiful sights of Montauk. This place was a photographer's dream.

"Smile," I spoke as I held the camera up for a selfie of me and Noah. I snapped the picture and then looked at the frame. It was perfect.

❦ 13 ❧

ONE MONTH LATER

N*oah*

Quinn and I grew closer every day and spent every night together. The nightmare I had been living the past twelve years had finally come to an end. I still hadn't told my parents yet and I knew it was a matter of time before they found out. My mother invited me to dinner, and I knew it was the right time to tell them both about Quinn.

"Hello, my sweet boy." My mother smiled as she kissed my cheek when I walked through the door.

"Hey, Mom."

"Hello, son," my father spoke. "Whiskey?"

"Sure. Just a small one, though."

"Are you feeling okay?" he asked with an arch in his brow.

"Yeah. I'm good."

My mother called us to the dining room table as dinner was served.

"It's been a while since we all had dinner together. I'm happy you could make it, Noah," my mother spoke.

"Thanks. Me too, Mom. Listen, there's something I need to tell you," I spoke with a nervous voice, not knowing how they were going to react.

"What is it, son? Is everything okay?" my dad asked.

"Yeah. Everything is great, actually. I've met someone, and we've been seeing each other for about a month."

"Oh my gosh, that's wonderful news." My mother beamed with excitement. "What's her name?"

I took in a deep breath.

"Mom, Dad, it's Quinn."

"Quinn Stevens?" My dad cocked his head.

"Yes."

"I don't understand," my mother spoke.

"She moved back to New York and we met at the art gallery event that we sponsored."

"Does she remember you?" my father asked.

"No, she doesn't remember. We talked, I took her to dinner, and we started seeing each other."

"Noah, did you at least tell her who you are?"

"No, and I don't know if I can."

"Son, you have to tell her. Your whole relationship is based on a lie right now. She was your girlfriend all those years ago. You know things she can't remember. Do you really think that's fair to her?"

"And what if she hates me and I lose her again? For the first time in twelve years, I feel alive again."

"Oh, Noah," my mother spoke with sadness.

"Wouldn't you rather have her hate you for telling the truth instead of her finding out on her own?" my father asked. "Believe me, son, you don't want her to find out on her own."

I sighed as I threw back my whiskey.

"We're happy and I want to bring her to Thanksgiving."

"Of course. She's more than welcome. My god, it will be so good to see her again. You know how much your father and I loved her."

Instead of going home, I went straight to Quinn's apartment. I needed to see her. I gave a lot of thought to what my parents said, and I couldn't keep it a secret anymore. She needed to know who I was and what we had all those years ago.

"Hey, you." She smiled as she opened the door. "How was dinner with your parents?"

"Boring business talk. I missed you." I wrapped my arms around her.

"I missed you too. Are you okay?"

She could sense something was off with me. She always could.

"There's something I need to tell you." I broke our embrace, placed my hands on each side of her face, and stared into her beautiful innocent eyes.

"What is it?"

I couldn't do it. We were so happy, and I was grateful that she was back in my life and I knew telling her would ruin everything. Call me selfish. I knew I was, but it was too much of a risk.

"Noah?" she asked with a worried look.

"I love you, Quinn." I smiled.

"I love you too, Noah." The corners of her mouth curved upwards.

"I'm ready, and if you are, I want us to be in a committed relationship."

"I'm definitely ready. Are you sure you are?" she asked with concern.

"I've never been so sure about anything in my life. I love you to the moon and back."

I kissed her passionately, swept her up in my arms, and carried her to the bedroom, where we made love and stayed for the rest of the night.

***

"Look what I found." She smiled as she took a picture from her nightstand.

It was the picture of her and her parents outside their house.

"I thought I lost it and have been trying to find it since I moved. It was stuck in between some sweaters I put away."

I was there. I was the one who took the picture when I dropped her off at home the night of the accident.

"It's a beautiful picture, Quinn. I'm happy you found it." I smiled.

"Me too. Look at that beautiful locket I'm wearing. I wish I still had it. My grandmother said that my parents gave it to me for my birthday and it got lost in the accident."

My heart started to ache as I swallowed the lump in my throat. I didn't know what to say to her except that I was sorry.

"At least I found the picture. I miss them, Noah."

"I know you do, baby." I held her tight.

14

Q*uinn*

Noah left for the office, and I grabbed a cup of coffee, opened my laptop, and Skyped Dr. Cooper.

"Hey, Quinn. It's been a while. I was starting to get worried."

"Hi, Dr. Cooper." I smiled. "I'm sorry. I've been really busy with work."

"And with Noah?" His brow raised.

"Yeah." I bit down on my bottom lip as the corners of my mouth curved upwards into a smile.

"So I take it the two of you are still seeing each other."

"We are and we're officially a couple now."

"Excellent. I'm happy to hear that. Have you told your grandmother yet?"

"No. Not yet. I will."

"I'm coming to New York to speak at some conferences. I'll be there for about a month. I'm hoping we can meet up."

"Yes! Definitely, Dr. Cooper. I can't wait for you to meet Noah."

"He sounds like a good man. I can't wait to meet him either."

"He's perfect, and I finally figured out why I felt the way I did when I first met him."

"You did?"

"He's my soulmate, Dr. Cooper. This relationship is different from any of the other ones I've been in. We connect and we fit so perfectly together. He makes me so happy. He's like the missing puzzle piece of my life."

"Maybe you're right, Quinn. Listen, sweetheart, I have to run. I have a patient coming in about two minutes."

"Okay. Give me a call or shoot me a text message when you're in New York."

"I will. Have a good day."

"You too, Dr. Cooper."

৩%৩

IT WAS THANKSGIVING AND I WAS SO EXCITED, BUT NERVOUS TO meet Noah's parents. We pulled up to his family home and I took in a deep breath.

"They're going to love you. Trust me." He squeezed my hand.

I gave him a smile as he helped me from the car and we walked hand in hand up to the front door. This house was just as big as the one in Montauk. As soon as Noah opened the door, an older woman appeared. She stared at me for a moment and I could sense she was just as nervous as I was.

"Mom, this is Quinn. Quinn, this is my mother Jane."

"Come here, gorgeous girl." She held out her arms for a hug.

"It's nice to meet you, Mrs. Kingston."

"You will call me Jane." She smiled.

"Hello, son. Happy Thanksgiving."

"Hi, Dad. Happy Thanksgiving. I want you to meet Quinn. Quinn, this is my father, Grant."

"It's nice to meet you, Mr. Kingston."

"Call me Grant, and the pleasure is all mine." He took hold of my hand and brought it up to his lips. "Can I get you a glass of wine?" he asked me.

"I got it, Dad." Noah smiled.

We walked into the living room and Noah poured us each a glass of wine.

"You have a lovely home," I said to Jane.

"Thank you. It's our pride and joy. Come with me. I'll give you the tour." She smiled.

I followed her into the massive kitchen first and then she took me upstairs.

"It's good to see Noah happy again," she spoke.

"He told me about his relationship he had with someone years ago and how it broke his heart, but he won't tell me anything else about it."

"That was the past, honey. He doesn't like to talk about it. All that matters now is that he's happy that you're in his life." She gave my hand a pat. "Let's go ask Pierre if dinner is ready."

Thanksgiving with his parents was great and I really liked them a lot. After we ate and talked some more, Noah and I headed back to his place.

I let out a long yawn. "I'm tired."

"Is that so?" he asked as his lips lightly brushed against mine. "Are you too tired for this?" He kissed me passionately. "Or this?" His hands reached under my dress and gave my ass a firm squeeze. "Or how about this?" His finger dipped inside me and I let out a moan. Just as I was getting full pleasure from him exploring me, he stopped, turned, and began to walk away.

"Excuse me? What are you doing?"

"You're tired, remember?" he spoke.

I ran after him and jumped on his back, wrapping my arms around his neck.

"I'm not tired anymore. You better finish what you started." I kissed his cheek.

"Are you sure you're up to it?" he asked as he carried me up the stairs.

"I'm more than up to it."

****

I rolled off him, my body dripping with sweat as I lay on my back and tried to catch my breath.

"Damn, Quinn. What got into you?" Noah asked, breathless as he smiled at me.

"You did. You got into me." I grinned as I looked over at him. "I told you I was up for it."

❧ 15 ❧

ONE WEEK LATER

Noah
    "Don't forget Dr. Cooper is coming over for dinner tonight," she spoke as she handed me a cup of coffee.

"I haven't forgotten, baby. Are you cooking or do you want me to hire someone?"

"I'm cooking." I lightly slapped him on the chest as I let out a light laugh.

"I thought you were, but I just wanted to make sure." I smirked. "I have to run. I'm going to be late for a meeting if I don't leave now."

I leaned in and kissed her beautiful soft lips.

"I love you to the moon and back, baby." I grinned.

"I love you too."

◈

AFTER MY MEETING WAS OVER, I MET HENRY FOR LUNCH AT THE Capital Grille.

"So, how is Quinn?" he asked.

"She's great. She's really great." I smiled.

"Have you decided when you're going to tell her?"

"No. Not yet." I sighed.

"Are you ever going to tell her?" he asked with an arch in his brow.

"Yeah, eventually."

"You know the longer you wait, the worse it'll be."

"Listen, Henry, let's change the subject. I don't want to talk about this. I know damn well I need to tell her, but I'll do it when I'm ready. Her therapist is coming over for dinner tonight. Maybe I can talk to him first and get his advice."

⚜

I WALKED INTO THE PENTHOUSE, SET MY BRIEFCASE DOWN, AND went into the kitchen, where Quinn was preparing dinner.

"Hey, baby." I smiled as I wrapped my arms around her.

"Hi. How was your day?" She kissed my lips.

"It was good. What are you making? It smells delicious in here."

"Homemade chicken pot pie. It's one of Dr. Cooper's favorites."

"Sounds good. I'm going to go change. I'll be back down in a minute and help you." I gave her lips a soft kiss.

After I changed out of my suit and into something more comfortable, the penthouse phone rang.

"Hello, Curtis," I answered.

"Good evening, Mr. Kingston. There is a Dr. Cooper here to see you and Quinn."

"Send him right up. Thank you."

Just as I was walking down the stairs, there was a knock on the door.

"Dr. Cooper, nice to meet you. I'm Noah Kingston." I extended my hand.

"Nice to finally meet you, Noah."

"Please come in."

"Dr. Cooper." Quinn smiled as she ran over and gave him a hug. "It's good to see you."

"Hello, Quinn." He grinned.

"The two of you go into the living room. Dinner will be ready soon," she spoke.

"Do you need any help?" I asked.

"Nope. I've got everything under control." She smiled.

I led Dr. Cooper into the living room and poured him a glass of scotch.

"I was wondering if you had some time tomorrow to meet. There's something I need to talk to you about," I spoke.

"What about?" he asked with concern.

"It's about Quinn."

"You know, Noah, I can't discuss anything with you. Doctor-patient confidentiality."

"I know that. There's something I need to tell her, and I would like your advice first."

"Okay." He pulled out his phone. "I can meet you at two p.m. tomorrow. Will that work?"

"Two o'clock is fine."

"Where would you like to meet? I can come to your office if it's more convenient."

"Sure. My office will be good. We'll have some privacy there."

***

"ELLEN, I HAVE A MEETING AT TWO O'CLOCK. CLEAR MY SCHEDULE because I'm not sure how long it's going to take," I spoke as I headed into my office.

"I know nothing about a meeting."

"I know you don't, because I scheduled it last night." I smirked.

It was exactly two o'clock on the dot when Ellen walked into my office with Dr. Cooper.

"Your appointment is here." She arched her brow at me.

"Thanks, Ellen. Hold all my calls. I don't want to be disturbed. Dr. Cooper." I extended my hand. "Good to see you again. Please have a seat." I gestured.

"Thank you, Noah," he spoke as he took the seat across from my desk. "So what is it you need my advice on?"

❧ 16 ❧

Noah

I sat down behind my desk and took in a deep breath.

"I honestly don't know where to start. You know I love Quinn."

"Yes, I can see that, and I can also see that she loves you too."

"There's something I need to tell her and I'm afraid it's going to ruin us."

"Okay. Tell me what it is, and I'll give you my opinion."

"What I'm about to tell you stays between us," I spoke.

"Of course. I understand." He nodded his head.

"I met Quinn when she had just turned sixteen. We connected instantly and we fell in love. We were in a relationship for over a year. She was and still is the love of my life. We had our whole future planned out. I was going off to Yale, and after she graduated high school, she was also going. We planned where we were going to live, when we'd get married, and how many kids we'd have. We never went a day without seeing each other, even if time wasn't on our side and we could only spend an hour together. Then the accident happened, and her grandmother told me that I needed to leave her alone, that she had a lot of healing to do, and since she lost the last five years of her life, I could no longer be a part of it. Then she took her back to Minnesota with her and I never saw her again."

He sat there and listened intently while his eye steadily narrowed.

"And now the two of you found each other again and everything is perfect, right?"

"Yes. After losing her, I became a changed man, and for the worse. I started drinking and sleeping around with any woman I could just to try and numb the pain of not being able to be with her."

"Quinn was a mess when she came to the hospital. She was enraged, defiant, and wouldn't listen to anyone. She was in such a bad place, but I got through to her and I helped her, and I will be there for her again when you tell her. Because, Noah, you have to tell her. You can't carry this burden for the rest of your life. It will eat you alive. Quinn has the right to know that you were a huge part of her life before the accident. What you're doing right now is deceiving her."

"She's going to hate me."

"I imagine she'll be upset and angry because you didn't tell her the moment you met her, but she'll eventually come around. She loves you. The way I saw her last night and when we Skype is a person I never saw before. Quinn is the happiest I've ever seen, and that's all because of you. When she told me that she had met you, she said she felt something inside of her that she'd never felt before. Even though her mind didn't remember you, her heart did." He smiled. "The heart is a powerful organ."

"I can't lose her again, Dr. Cooper. It'll destroy me."

"It will destroy you if you don't tell her. Quinn is a strong woman. She survived a great tragedy and she'll survive this as well. Her grandmother gave you no choice."

"I could have stayed and fought for her."

"Fought for what? She didn't remember you. Both her parents were dead and the only person she knew was her grandmother. You were nothing but a complete stranger to her at that point. Do you believe that after all she'd been through, she would just accept you were a part of her life and greet you with open arms? You left because you loved her enough to let her go and heal."

"But I could have prevented her from trying to kill herself. I could have helped her."

"You don't know that. Not being able to remember five years of your life is very hard on a person. In fact, you could have made things worse for her."

"And now I'm about to do that," I spoke as I leaned back in my chair.

"Listen, Noah. The love you two share is rare and a love like that just doesn't die. The two of you were meant to be together, and even after twelve years, she fell in love with you all over again. I'd call that fate, my friend. You can't put this off any longer. You need to tell her before something happens and she finds out on her own. And, to be fair, I will be here for you as well." He smiled. "I'm in New York for the next month."

"Thank you, Dr. Cooper. I appreciate it. And thank you for everything you've done for Quinn. I will forever be indebted to you."

"You're welcome." He got up from his seat and extended his hand. "Do what's right."

I lightly shook his hand and walked him out of my office.

❧ 17 ☙

Quinn

I finished a photoshoot in Central Park and then headed back to Noah's penthouse. I practically lived there now with as much time as I spent there, which was fine with me. I loved his penthouse. I set my bag down on the counter and walked into the laundry room to grab the basket of clothes I needed to put away. Taking it upstairs and into the bedroom, I set it down on the bed and took my clothes out one by one and neatly folded them. When I was done, I folded Noah's clean socks that were sitting in a basket in the corner of the bedroom. Opening his sock drawer, it was a disaster, which I was surprised for him being so meticulous about everything else. I started to organize his drawer, when I came across a small box. I stared at it. I should have just shut the drawer and walked away, but I couldn't. I needed to see what was in that box. Was it a gift for me? Perhaps a Christmas gift? I placed my hand on the box and then quickly removed it. I shouldn't. I should. I was excited, but I knew it was wrong. He'd never know. It would be my secret, and when he gave it to me, I'd act totally surprised. I took the box from the drawer and sat down on the bed. I'd just take a peek and put it back in its place.

I removed the lid and sat there as my mind was confused and my heart started racing as to what sat inside. I grabbed the chain and pulled out the silver heart pendant and held it up in front of me. It looked like the same necklace my parents had given me, except there was an empty space in the middle. Something had fallen out and the clasp was broken. I started to tremble as I opened the locket and looked inside.

I will always love you to the moon and back.

I sat there for what seemed like hours, in a trance, staring at the locket I held in my hand. He wouldn't have bought this for me with a missing piece and a broken clasp. I heard the front door open and Noah calling my name, but I couldn't move.

"There you—"

He stopped mid-sentence as he walked into the room. I looked up at him and held open my hand, revealing the locket.

"What is this, Noah? Why do you have this?"

He sighed as he placed his hand on the back of his head.

"We need to talk, Quinn," he spoke with seriousness as he began to walk towards the bed.

"Stay right where you are. Please."

He stopped and stared at me with fear in his eyes.

"Answer my question. What is this? I had one just like it that my parents gave me. It looks exactly like the same one except the clasp is broken and there's a missing piece," I spoke as tears filled my eyes.

"Please, baby. Let me sit next to you. I'll explain everything."

"No!" I shouted. "You will explain now from right where you're standing."

"That is your necklace, but your parents didn't give it to you. I did. I gave it to you the night of the accident."

"What?" I cocked my head as the tears began to stream down my face.

"Damn it!" he shouted. "You and I were together. We met in Kingston's Department Store when you had just turned sixteen. We were together for over a year before the accident." Tears filled his eyes.

"No. That's not true. My grandmother said I wasn't seeing anyone. She said I wasn't interested in boys because I was focused on school and photography. You're lying to me."

"She's the liar!" he yelled. "The night of the accident, you had gone to dinner with your parents for their anniversary. You wanted me to go, but I couldn't because I had that damn board meeting with my father. The hospital called me because I was your emergency contact. I rushed over there, and you were in surgery. The doctor had told me about your parents, and I gave them your grandmother's number. Then you woke up and didn't remember the last five years of your life. It destroyed me, Quinn, because what we have now, we had then. We were so in love and we had our whole future planned out. I was going off to Yale in a couple of weeks and after you graduated high school, you were going too to study photography. We were going to get an apartment and live together. I gave you that necklace and told you that it was my heart and that I'd always be with you when we couldn't be together."

I gasped for air as I sat there and listened to him. My heart was pounding out of my chest and I felt like I was going to pass out.

"I don't believe you." I looked up at him. "You would have told me when we first met. You're lying!" I yelled.

He walked over to the closet and pulled a small box down that was hidden in the corner up on the shelf. He removed the lid and handed me a picture.

"You took that picture of us in Central Park and gave it to me for my birthday."

I stared at the picture and then back at him as a memory flashed through my mind.

"Oh my god. It was you. You were the one who came into my hospital room after the accident and gave me the roses."

"I couldn't leave until I knew for sure that you had no memory of me."

"For years I had tried to remember things about those five years. When I moved back here, I'd look at people on the street and in the stores with the hopes that someone would recognize me and could help me fill in the pieces. You knew this whole time and you didn't tell me!" I screamed as I stood up from the bed.

"I was too afraid to tell you and I was afraid you wouldn't have believed me."

"The story you told me about the relationship all those years ago was with me."

"Damn right it was, and after that, I changed into a person I never want to be again. I drank too much and slept around just to try to forget you. I was miserable and out of control. I was in a dark place, Quinn. Then I saw you again and all that darkness lifted. I felt like I could breathe again."

"I can't do this. My head is so confused. You lied to me this whole time, Noah. You led me to believe that we were strangers. You had information about my past that you kept from me. Who the fuck does that? I need to get out of here. I can't be near you."

"Quinn, don't!" he shouted as tears streamed down his face and he grabbed hold of my arm. "We can talk about this."

"You should have thought about that the day we met at the art gallery. I trusted you with my heart and soul."

I grabbed my purse and my laptop from the dresser, ran down the stairs, and flew out the front door. Hailing a cab, I took it to my apartment. I was hysterical and a mess. I couldn't believe this and I couldn't think straight. I grabbed my suitcase from my closet and started throwing clothes into it as fast as I could. I opened my laptop and searched for the next flight out to Minnesota. There was one leaving JFK in two hours with three seats available. I booked it, flew out the door, and hailed a cab to the airport.

❧ 18 ❧

N^{oah} I was sick to my stomach as I lay on the bed. I knew this would happen. I sat up and placed my face in the palm of my hands, letting the tears fall from my eyes at the fact that she hated me. Once I composed myself, I went downstairs, grabbed the bottle of whiskey, and drank the whole damn thing until I passed out on the couch. When I awoke in the middle of the night, I grabbed another bottle and drank that until I passed out again. I needed to numb the pain that tore through me.

"Noah. Noah," I heard a voice say as I was being shaken.

Opening my eyes, I saw Ellen standing over me.

"Go away, Ellen," I moaned as I placed my arm over my forehead.

"I will do no such thing. It is twelve o'clock. Do you know how worried I was? You didn't show up at the office, you didn't call, and you weren't answering your phone. You're lucky I didn't mention this to your father. Now get your drunk ass up. I'm going to make you some coffee."

"I don't want coffee."

"Too bad. You're drinking it, even if I have to force it down your throat, and then you're going to tell me what the hell is going on."

A few moments later, Ellen returned and forced me to sit up. My head was pounding as she handed me a glass of water and some aspirin.

"Take these now!" she commanded.

I grabbed them from her hand, but not without giving her a dirty look, and tossed them down the back of my throat.

"Good boy. Now drink your coffee," she spoke as she sat down next to me. "Where's Quinn, Noah?"

"I don't know. She left."

"You told her, didn't you?"

"Not of my own free will. She found the locket in my drawer and things just escalated from there. She hates me, Ellen, just like I knew she would."

"All of this could have been avoided if you were just honest with her from the start."

I put up my hand to her because I didn't want to hear it.

"You should have seen her. She was crying and yelling at me. She called me a liar."

"She was in shock. Once she calms down and can properly assess everything, she'll be back."

"I doubt it. Clear my schedule for the next few days. I'm not coming in. Tell my father I'm sick or something."

"Work would be the best thing for you right now. It'll keep your mind off her."

"Nothing in this world could keep my mind off her. Not even twelve years of not seeing her."

"Go take a shower and sober up, Noah," she spoke as she got up from the couch. "You reek of whiskey."

"Thanks, Ellen," I spoke with sarcasm.

"By the way, go talk to that doctor friend of yours," she said as she walked out the door.

I laid my head back and sighed. I grabbed my phone from the table and looked at it, hoping I had a message from Quinn, but there was nothing. I destroyed her. I destroyed us, and I didn't think I could handle it. I hated how she left and how I didn't know if she was okay. I set my coffee cup down on the table and closed my eyes.

❦ 19 ❦

Q   *uinn*

        I was angry. Hurt and angry. Not only at Noah, but at my grandmother for lying to me all those years. I felt betrayed by both of them and I needed answers.

"Quinn, oh my goodness, what are you doing here?" my grandmother asked as she placed her hands on each side of my face.

"Hi, Grandma. I just thought it was time for a visit since I didn't see you for Thanksgiving."

"Why didn't you call and tell me?" she asked as she grabbed my suitcase from me.

"I wanted to surprise you." I smiled.

"Well, this is definitely a surprise. Come to the kitchen and I'll make us some tea. Are you hungry?" she asked.

"No. I ate on the plane."

I heard my phone ding in my pocket, so I pulled it out and there was a text message from Noah.

"No matter what happens, I will always love you to the moon and back, Quinn Stevens. I'm sorry."

The ache in my heart intensified as I slowly set down my phone.

"Grandma, I met someone in New York."

"You did?" She smiled as she grabbed the tea kettle from the stove and poured hot water into our cups.

"Yeah, and I'm in love with him. We've been seeing each other for a while now. I'm sorry I didn't tell you before. I just wanted to be sure."

"Quinn, that's wonderful. What's his name and what does he do?"

Moment of truth.

"His name is Noah Kingston and he works for his family's company, Kingston International. They own Kingston's Department Store in Manhattan."

As she went to put the tea kettle back on the stove, she froze, and I studied her with a narrowed eye.

"Wow. That's great, Quinn," she spoke in a shaky voice.

"The moment I met him, I knew. I'd never felt anything like it before."

"How did the two of you meet?" she asked as she handed me my cup.

"We met at the art gallery. The one where I had my photographs displayed."

"I see."

"I've never been happier, Grandma. Have I?" I stared directly into her eyes.

"You were always a happy child, Quinn."

"Was I this happy before the accident? See, I wouldn't know because I can't remember anything and I depended on you to help me fill in the gaps, but all you said was some bullshit about school and photography."

"Don't you dare curse in my home," she angrily spoke.

"And don't you dare sit there and lie to me."

I reached into my pocket and pulled out the locket.

"I found this in his drawer." I placed it on the table.

"What's that?" she asked.

"The locket he gave me the night of the accident. The same locket you gave back to him before you made him leave."

"Quinn, you don't understand."

I slammed my fist down on the table and she flinched.

"You're wrong! What I understand now is that you've been lying to me all these years!" I shouted as tears filled my eyes.

"You were in a horrible accident, you lost five years of your life and your parents. You didn't need him. You didn't remember him. He was leaving for Yale and he had his whole life ahead of him. You needed to heal from everything that happened, and you didn't need the added stress of not being able to remember who he was. I told him if he truly loved you, he would let you go, and I don't apologize for that."

"Who were you to make that decision?" I asked through gritted teeth.

"Your grandmother. The one that was responsible for your well-being. You were still a minor. Besides, you needed to come back to Minnesota with me, and like I said, he was going off to Yale. It was for everyone's best interest."

Anger tore through me.

"I'm assuming since you found the locket, he didn't tell you either. He failed to mention who he was. Was he ever going to tell you? Or just keep it a secret for the rest of his life?" she asked with a smug look and an arch in her brow.

I took in a deep breath and a sip of my tea.

"I don't know. Grandma." I calmed myself, reached over, and placed my hand on hers. "You knew us; how could you keep something like that from me?" I begged for an answer.

"It seemed like the right decision at the time. That's why I was so against you moving back to New York. I was afraid you'd run into him and he'd tell you everything and then you'd hate me. But I guess I didn't have to worry about that because he didn't tell you himself."

I sat there and stared at her as shock swept across my face.

"What about my bedroom? I'm sure I had photos of us, and my phone?"

"Your phone was crushed in the accident. You know that. As for your room, I went and cleaned it out before you got out of the hospital. I threw away all the pictures of the two of you and everything he had given you. I erased any sign of him being in your life."

"My god, how could you?" I shook my head in disbelief as I held up my hand. "You saw how I was. I tried to kill myself, and you could have prevented that by telling me about him."

"And you think me telling you about a boy would have prevented that? No, Quinn, it wouldn't have. You were in your own desolate world. You barely spoke, you barely ate, and you barely went out. Me telling you about him would have only made matters worse because you couldn't remember who he was, and you would have been fighting yourself to remember, and that would have only made you more depressed."

I stared into her unapologetic, cold eyes.

"You know what, maybe you're right. I'm not talking about this anymore. I came here to get answers and you sure as hell gave them to me. My mom would be so disappointed in you right now." I shook my head as I got up from the table.

"Where are you going?" she asked.

"I'm leaving. I can't stay here. Goodbye, Grandma."

"Quinn, don't you dare walk out that door!" she shouted.

I grabbed my suitcase from the foyer and left.

❧ 20 ❧

Q*uinn*
        I opened my eyes and looked at my watch. My flight
was leaving in an hour. I'd spent the night in the airport
after my previous flight to New York was cancelled due to weather
conditions. I got up from my seat, grabbed my purse, and found the
nearest restroom. I splashed my face with cold water and stared at
myself in the mirror. Reaching into my purse, I pulled out my powder
and dusted my face with it, trying to make myself look somewhat less
distraught. I ran a brush through my brown locks, grabbed a rubber
band, and pulled my hair back into a ponytail.

"That'll have to do for now," I said to myself.

I walked out of the bathroom and found the nearest place for a cup
of coffee before I boarded the plane. As I was standing in line with all
the other people whose flights got canceled last night, I felt a tap on
my shoulder. When I turned around, I was shocked to see Henry
standing there.

"It is you." He smiled.

"Henry? What are you doing here?" We lightly hugged.

"I'm on my way back to New York. My firm sent me here for a

business conference. What about you? I had no idea you were in Minnesota."

"I wasn't here long. Not even twenty-four hours."

It was my turn to order and Henry stepped in, ordered his at the same time, and paid for my coffee.

"You don't have to buy me coffee."

"I know I don't have to. I want to." He grinned. "I've been trying to get hold of Noah and he's not returning my calls or text messages."

I took in a deep breath.

"I left him."

"What?" He cocked his head in shock.

We both grabbed our coffees from the counter and walked to our gate.

"We got into a huge fight."

"Man, I'm sorry, Quinn."

"What seat are you?" I asked him.

"I'm in first class. Seat 2C. How about you?"

"I'm in first class too. Seat 4D. My flight was canceled last night, so when they put me on this flight, I got an upgrade."

"Very cool." He grinned.

They called first class for boarding, so Henry and I boarded the plane and took our seats. A few moments later, a nice old lady took her seat next to me. I gave her a small smile.

"Excuse me, ma'am," Henry spoke as he walked over to us. "Would you mind if we switched seats?"

"I'm fine right where I'm at," she said.

"Pretty please. I have a nice window seat in row two."

"Why do you want to switch?" she asked as she glared at him.

"I just met this beautiful woman sitting next to you and I would love to get to know her better. But that would be pretty difficult since I'm up there and she's back here." He graciously smiled.

She looked at him and then at me.

"Would you like him to sit here or do you want me to beat him off with my cane?"

I couldn't help but let out a laugh.

"I wouldn't mind at all if he sat next to me."

"Very well." She began to get up from her seat and Henry reached over to help her. "Hands off, son. I can get up myself."

"Gee," Henry said as he took the seat next to me. "So what did you and Noah fight about?"

"I really don't want to talk about it. I'm sure he'll tell you."

"He told you, didn't he?"

I stared at him in shock.

"You knew about me?"

Henry reached over and grabbed my hand.

"Quinn, I've known about you since the first day Noah and I met in college. I had to kick and save his ass a few times. That man was so heartbroken."

"He should have told me right from the very beginning."

"You're right. He should have, but he was battling his own fears."

"I don't care." I turned and looked out the window.

"You're hurt. I get that, but you didn't experience the pain Noah did for the last twelve years because you had no memory of him. I have never in my life seen someone so broken over a girl before. That night he saw you for the first time in the art gallery, he had to rush out of there to get some fresh air because he felt like he couldn't breathe. He loves you, Quinn. And the fact that you met again after twelve years isn't coincidental. The fact that you fell in love with him all over again isn't coincidental. It's fate. Plain and simple. I don't care if you don't believe in that shit or not. I'm not a huge believer myself, but in this case, I believe it."

"Thanks, Henry." I gave his hand a squeeze.

"Noah is a different man since you came back into his life. A man I didn't know, and a man I would like to keep around." He smirked.

"I still have a lot of thinking to do. He lied to me."

"See, that's where I have to correct you. He didn't lie to you, Quinn. He just didn't tell you. Now if he would have told you that you'd never met before, that would be a lie. Really think about that."

"How are you still single?" I softly smiled.

"Haven't found the right girl yet, I suppose."

We landed at JFK and Henry was kind enough to drive me home. After I thanked him, I went up to my apartment and took my suitcase to my room. It felt good to be back in New York. This was my true home.

❧ 21 ❧

ONE WEEK LATER

Q*uinn*
        I didn't leave my apartment the whole week. All I did was work and think about Noah and this whole situation. I hadn't talked to my grandmother, even though she kept calling me for a couple of days after I got back. Christmas was approaching, and I hadn't done a single thing. Maybe tomorrow I would go out and get a small tree. I wasn't really in the Christmas spirit. Maybe I'd just skip it this year.

It was nine o'clock at night when my door buzzer went off. I went over to the intercom and pressed the button.

"Hello."

"Quinn." I heard a low voice.

"Noah?"

"Yeah. It's me," he slurred.

"What are you doing here?"

He didn't answer.

"Noah?"

I sighed, grabbed my coat from the closet, put on my slippers, and went downstairs. When I opened the building door, I found him in a sitting position against the wall on the cold cement.

"Noah." I ran over to him.

He mumbled something, and I couldn't understand him. He was drunk.

"Where's your coat? My god, it's freezing out here."

I grabbed his arm, hooked it around my neck, and lifted him up. I walked him inside the building and over to the elevator.

"I'm sorry," he slurred.

"Save it for when you're sober," I said.

I dragged him down the hall, into my apartment, and straight to the bedroom, where I sat him on the bed. I took off his shoes and then went into my closet and grabbed one of his sweatshirts I had taken from his house.

"Arms up, Noah. We have to get this shirt off you."

"I love you so much, Quinn."

"I know. Just be quiet and get into bed," I spoke as I pulled the sweatshirt over his head and then pulled back the covers. "Sleep it off and we'll talk in the morning."

I walked out of the bedroom and went into the kitchen to pour a glass of wine. I couldn't believe he was passed out drunk in my bed. I took my wine and stood in the doorway of my bedroom and stared at him. A small smile crossed my lips as he lay there and slept. Henry was right. None of this was a coincidence. If I could love him this much now, I certainly had to have loved him back then. There was no denying the instant attraction or feeling I felt when I first saw him. Like Dr. Cooper said, "My mind didn't remember, but my heart did."

The next morning, before I climbed out of bed, I placed my hand on Noah's heart to make sure he was still alive. He didn't move or make a sound all night and a part of me was worried. I popped a k-cup in the Keurig and watched as the coffee streamed into the cup. Once it was finished, I took the cup into the bedroom and sat Indian-style on the bed, waiting for him to wake up. A few moments later, he stirred, and a groan erupted from him as he slowly opened his eyes.

"Quinn?" he whispered. "How—"

"You showed up at my door last night drunk off your ass. You don't remember?"

"No. The last thing I remembered was leaving the bar. Shit. My head," he moaned as he placed his arm over his eyes.

"I'll go get you some aspirin. Here's some coffee to get you started."

I went into the bathroom and shook two aspirin into my hand. I grabbed the bottle of water from the nightstand and handed it to him.

"Thanks." He threw the aspirin into his mouth and chased them down with water. "I'll get going." He began to climb out of bed.

I reached over and grabbed his arm.

"Get back into bed."

He looked down at my hand and then up at me.

"Is that an order?"

"Yeah. Actually, it is an order. When you're feeling better, we can talk. I have to run to the post office and mail some photographs. I'll be back in a while. Get some more rest."

"Okay." A light smile splayed across his face.

I put on my shoes, grabbed my purse, and headed to the post office. It took longer than I anticipated because the line was so long. When I arrived back at my apartment, Noah emerged from the bedroom, freshly showered and in some casual clothes.

"Hi," he spoke.

"Hi. Sorry it took me so long. The line at the post office was ridiculous."

"That's okay."

Things felt awkward between us, and I knew he felt it too.

"Thanks for letting me stay here last night. I'm really sorry that I just showed up like that."

"You're welcome. I'd never seen you like that before," I said.

"I know and I'm sorry you had to. I didn't intend to come here. So how are you?" he asked as he tucked his hands into his pants pockets.

"I'm fine. Would you like some more coffee? I could go for some."

"Sure." He smiled.

I turned to the Keurig and placed a k-cup inside.

"I went to Minnesota and saw my grandmother."

"I know. Henry mentioned he saw you at the airport and you two sat next to each other on the plane."

"Yeah. It was a nice surprise."

"How is your grandmother doing?"

I took the cup from the Keurig and set it on the island for him. He slowly walked over and picked it up.

"She's okay, I guess. I don't know what to say about her except that I'm sorry for the things she said to you."

"You don't need to apologize for her. I think she believed she was doing the right thing."

"It wasn't her choice to make," I spoke as I took my cup and brought it up to my lips. "Just explain to me why you didn't tell me. I know what you said before, but I just need you to say it again."

"Of course."

We stood on opposite sides of the island as we stared into each other's eyes.

"I didn't want to tell you that night I met you at the gallery because there would have been no point if you didn't find yourself attracted to me. Then we went out and I knew you felt something. The more time we spent together, the more complicated it became. I was so afraid that if I told you, I'd upset you and you'd hate me. But, believe me, Quinn, I was going to tell you. I just needed to find the right time. I was all set to tell you that night I told you that I loved you. But I couldn't. When I told that I had something to tell you, I saw the fear in your eyes. The last thing I ever wanted to do was hurt you."

"What were we like back then?"

The corners of his mouth curved upwards. "We were exactly how we are now, or were, before all of this. It was love at first sight. You bent down to try and pick up the glass from the vase you knocked over at the department store, and the moment I grabbed hold of your wrist to stop you and you looked up at me with those eyes, I knew you were the one for me. I asked you to dinner that night and you agreed. I took you to Carbone and we never spent a day apart from that night on. We had the best year of our lives. I took you to my prom and you wore a beautiful long red dress. Afterwards, instead of going to some dumb prom party, I had Sean take us to Central Park, where we spread a blanket on the ground and laid together and looked up at the stars while we talked about our future."

I reached over and placed my hand on his.

"When I first met you, I had this overwhelming feeling in my heart that I couldn't explain. I had only known you a few moments, but I felt like I had known you forever. In my mind, you were a complete stranger, but my heart, it knew exactly who you were," I softly spoke.

"I never wanted to leave you, Quinn. I was going to stay and put Yale off until you got better. But your grandmother didn't give me a choice."

"I know, Noah. She told me everything."

"Do you forgive me?" he quietly asked. "I'm so sorry I didn't tell you."

I stood there for a moment and stared into his apologetic eyes. How could I not forgive him? I loved him and he deserved a second chance. We deserved a second chance. I walked around the island and over to where he stood and wrapped my arms around him.

"Yes. I forgive you and I love you," I whispered.

He held me close as he picked me up. My legs wrapped tightly around his waist and he nestled his face in my hair.

"I will always love you to the moon and back, Quinn Stevens."

❧ 22 ❧

N^{oah}

Noah I inhaled a sharp breath as the warmth inside her soothed my throbbing cock. My hands fondled her breasts as I steadily thrust in and out of her, making her moan with each long stroke. She grabbed the headboard with one hand and threw her head back as an orgasm tore through her beautiful body. I wrapped my hand around hers and halted as I exploded inside her, moaning at the pleasure that filled me. I looked into her eyes before pressing my lips against hers. My heart was racing at the speed of light as I collapsed on top of her and our bodies melted together. We both lay there, trying to catch our breath.

"You are amazing." I smiled as I brought my lips to hers.

"No, you're the one who's amazing." She nipped at my lower lip.

I rolled off her and onto my back. Suddenly, Quinn climbed out of bed.

"Where do you think you're going?" I asked with a smile.

"To take a bath. Care to join me?" Her brow raised as a sexy sinful smile crossed her lips.

She walked into the bathroom and started the water while I went into the kitchen and poured us each a glass of wine. Quinn twisted up her hair as I climbed into the bubbly hot water. She climbed in between my legs and laid her back against my chest as the water covered us. This was my bliss.

"Christmas is coming," I spoke. "Neither one of us has a tree yet. I was thinking we could go get one."

"My place or yours?" She beamed with excitement.

"We could get one for each place. Unless you would like to just come stay at my place, like forever." I grinned.

"Are you asking me to move in with you?" she asked as she lifted her head and looked up at me.

"Yes. This is how it was supposed to be, Quinn."

"What about my lease? I can't break it."

"You won't have to. My company will take over the lease. We're always putting people up in apartments when we bring them over from other states or countries to work for us."

"You're serious?" A grin crossed her face.

"I'm definitely serious. I want my penthouse to be our penthouse, our home."

"Then after our bath, let's get dressed and go Christmas tree shopping for *our* home."

I smiled as I leaned down, and our lips met one more time. After our bath, we got dressed and headed out the door.

⚜

"How big of a tree do you usually get?" she asked as we walked around the Christmas tree lot.

"I don't know. I've never put one up in the penthouse."

"What?" She laughed. "Why not?"

"I never wanted to celebrate Christmas without you. It meant nothing to me anymore."

"Noah." She placed her hand on my cheek.

"But all that's changed now. Which one do you like? You can have any tree you want."

"To be honest, I'm not a fan of real trees. We had one once when I was a kid and my mom said never again. So we got an artificial tree and it became part of our home every year."

"I know." I smiled. "You and I decorated it our first Christmas together."

"We did?"

"We did." I placed my forehead against hers. "Let's go get our own tree that will become a part of our home every year."

"I'd love that." She crinkled her nose.

"I know the perfect place we can find one." I grinned.

We hailed a cab over to my department store.

"You can't be serious?" Quinn grinned as she looked out the window of the cab.

"We have some of the most beautiful trees."

"But they're displays and already decorated." She laughed.

"Doesn't matter. We'll find one we like and have it undecorated."

We walked into the department store, and instantly, I was greeted by all the employees on the first floor. We walked around and looked at all the trees on display until we both found a fourteen-foot pre-lit spruce that housed over two thousand clear lights.

"I love this one!" Quinn exclaimed.

"Me too. This one is brand new this year. It's only been up a couple of weeks. Shall we make this our tree?" I asked as I hooked my arm around her.

"Definitely. But what's your father going to say?"

"He'll be okay with it. In fact, he probably won't ever know."

I held up my finger to Trey, one of our store managers.

"Yes, Mr. Kingston?"

"I'm going to take this tree, so please have it undecorated and sent to my penthouse tomorrow morning around ten o'clock."

"Excuse me? You're *taking* this tree?" he asked in confusion.

"Yes," I replied as I arched my brow at him.

"I love that tree skirt," Quinn spoke.

"And we're taking the tree skirt as well."

"Very well, sir. We'll have it to you tomorrow morning. May I ask what you would like us to replace it with?"

"I'll have Ellen send another tree over. I'm sure there's more in storage somewhere. Thanks, Trey." I grinned as I patted him on the back.

I took hold of Quinn's hand and laced our fingers together as we walked out of the department store.

"Noah," she said as we walked down the street.

"Yeah, baby?"

"I want you to tell me more about the things we did when we were together."

I glanced over at her and she looked up at me with her baby blue eyes and a smile fixed on her face.

"I'd like to show you. There's something we used to do every Saturday in the winter together." I held up my hand and hailed us a cab.

"Where to?" the cab driver asked.

"Rockefeller Center."

"Rockefeller Center?" she asked. "What did we do there?"

"You'll see." A smirk crossed my lips.

We climbed out of the cab and went inside Rockefeller Center. Holding her hand, I led her to the Skate House.

"Ice skating?" She cocked her head at me. I haven't been on skates since I was a kid."

"Correction, you haven't been on skates since you were seventeen years old."

I bought our general admission tickets and rented our skates. It was a perfect crisp night and the snow was lightly falling.

"I don't know if I remember how to skate," she said with concern.

"I'll be holding on to you the whole time. I won't let you fall, Quinn. I didn't back then, and I won't now."

After lacing up our skates, I grabbed her hand and we slowly made our way onto the ice. I could tell she was nervous, so I held on tight. She wobbled a bit, but after a few moments, she found her rhythm and we glided across the ice together. I wrapped my arms around her from behind and we skated in unison. When we were done, I took our skates back up to the counter, grabbed her hand, and led her out of Rockefeller Center.

"That was fun!" She grinned as her lips met my cheek.

"We aren't finished yet. Every Saturday night, after we skated, we did one more thing."

"What?"

"You'll see."

We walked down the street to Betty Lou's, a small diner that served the best hot chocolate and pie in New York City. When we walked through the door, Betty Lou was standing behind the counter holding a pot of coffee. She looked at us with a shocked expression and slowly set the coffee pot back on its burner.

"Noah, is that...?"

"Yeah, Betty Lou. It's her."

She covered her face with her hands and walked over to us.

"Quinn. Look at you. You're all grown up," she spoke with tears in her eyes as she gave her a hug. "I know you don't remember me, darling, and that's okay."

"I'm so sorry," Quinn spoke.

"Nonsense. It's not your fault. Don't ever apologize for something that isn't your fault."

She looked over at the booth where Quinn and I used to sit every Saturday night.

"Hey, you two, I need to move you to another booth. This one is reserved for two special people," she spoke as she grabbed the menus from their hands and took them to another table. We sat down, and Quinn looked at me in confusion.

"This is where we came every Saturday night after ice skating. We'd sit at this table, order two hot chocolates and two slices of warm apple pie."

❧ 23 ❧

Quinn

Noah was sound asleep, his arm wrapped securely around me as I lay there on my side and tears streamed down my face. Anger consumed me. I carefully climbed out from under his arm and went down to the kitchen for a glass of water. Rage reared its ugly head as I screamed, threw the glass at the wall, and then grabbed the side of my head with my hands. Within seconds, Noah was in the kitchen. He looked at me and then at the shattered glass that lay in a puddle of water on the floor.

"Quinn, what's wrong?"

I fell to my knees, holding my head as a waterfall of tears poured from my eyes. Noah ran over to me, got down on the floor, and wrapped his arms around me.

"It's okay, baby." He stroked my hair.

"No!" I cried. "It's not okay."

He broke our embrace and placed his hands on each side of my face, wiping away my tears with his thumbs.

"Talk to me. Tell me what's wrong," his panicked voice spoke.

"I hate this. I hate you!" I pushed him, and he fell back, staring at me with fear in his eyes.

"Quinn."

"I hate you because you have all these memories of us and I have nothing! I tried so hard to remember and I couldn't. I have nothing," I spoke in a soft voice as I placed my face in my hands. "It isn't fair. I want to remember my life with you," I cried.

"It doesn't matter, baby."

"It does matter! It matters to me!" I shouted.

"Look at me," he said.

I couldn't.

"I said look at me!" he shouted in a stern voice.

I removed my hands from my face and looked at him with my tear-filled eyes. He moved closer to me and placed his hands on each side of my face.

"Do you remember the first time you saw me at the art gallery?" he asked.

I slowly nodded my head.

"Do you remember our first date?"

I nodded my head again.

"Do you remember me telling you how much I love you?"

"Yes," I quietly spoke.

"Do you remember me spilling orange juice all over my brand new suit because you didn't put the cap back on tight and I shook it?"

I nodded with a smile.

"That's all you need to remember, baby. The memories of now are what's important. The memories you and I have made every day since the night we met in the art gallery. The only thing that matters is we found each other again. That's all. We can't live in the past because we have our now and our future to look forward to."

"I'm sorry."

"Don't be." He pulled me into him and held me tight.

He pulled me up with him and then swooped me in his arms and carried me up the stairs while my head rested on his chest. He gently laid me down on the bed and climbed in next to me.

"I'm sorry I told you that I hated you. I didn't mean it," I said as I lightly stroked his chest. "I could never hate you."

"I know you didn't mean it. You're angry and I can understand that." He kissed the top of my head.

⚜

THE NEXT MORNING, THE CHRISTMAS TREE WAS DELIVERED promptly at ten o'clock and Noah and I agreed to decorate it later that night. He had to go into the office, and I had some errands to run. I was walking down Fifth Avenue, when I saw Dr. Cooper walking towards me.

"Quinn." He smiled.

"Hi, Dr. Cooper. Doing a little shopping?"

"I am. And you?"

"Yeah. I picked up some stockings for me and Noah," I said as I held up the white bag.

"Very nice. How have you been since our last chat?"

"I've been great, except I had a breakdown last night. A pretty bad one. I threw a glass of water at the kitchen wall." I bit my bottom lip.

"Okay." He looked at his watch. "I've got some time. How about we grab some lunch and talk about it."

"That would be great."

He held out his arm and I hooked mine around it, telling him what happened as we walked down the street.

"We had this amazing evening. We went ice skating just like we used to and then Noah took me to this diner where we ordered hot chocolate and apple pie. He was telling me the things we used to do, and I loved hearing it. Except later that night, out of the clear blue, something inside me just snapped. I told him that I hated him because he had all these memories of us, and I had nothing."

"And what did Noah say?"

"He calmed me down and kept asking me if I remembered all these things since we met at the art gallery. He said those memories are what matter now."

"He's right. All your memories aren't lost, Quinn. Whether you believe it or not. You've told me for years that you wanted to move back to New York, that you felt like there was a reason you felt so

86

strongly about it. You felt it with your heart and your soul, just like when you and Noah met again. See where I'm going with this?" He smiled.

"I knew that the missing piece of my life was here, didn't I?"

"I believe you did, and when the time was right and the opportunity presented itself, you followed your heart, and it led you back to where you belong. Right into the arms of Noah Kingston."

"Thanks, Dr. Cooper." I gave him a hug.

"You're welcome, sweetheart."

The two of us had lunch and continued our conversation. When we finished, I headed home.

❧ 24 ❧

Noah
I was walking down the hallway to my office, when I saw my father walking towards me.

"You got a minute, son?" he asked.

"Sure. Come on in, Dad."

We stepped into my office and I shut the door.

"What's up?" I asked as I took a seat behind my desk.

"I was just over at Kingston's and I noticed the fourteen-foot Christmas tree was missing. I asked Trey about it and he hesitantly said that you had it delivered to your house," he spoke with a raised brow.

"I did. Quinn and I needed a Christmas tree and we liked that one. What were you doing over there?"

"Looking around. It is my store."

"Well, the tree looks better in my penthouse." I smirked.

"That's fine, but you need to replace it."

"Ellen is working on a replacement right now. Don't worry, Dad."

"Well, I'm happy to see that you finally got your Christmas spirit back."

"Me too, Dad. Me too."

I finished my last meeting of the day and went home. When I walked through the door, Quinn came running into the foyer.

"I bought us something today." She smiled brightly.

"You did?" I grinned as I set my briefcase down and kissed her lips.

She grabbed my hand and led me into the living room and over to the fireplace, where two stockings with our names hung on the mantel.

"I love them."

I hooked my arm around her and kissed the side of her head. Looking around, I noticed the entire penthouse was decorated for Christmas.

"Did you do all this yourself?" I asked.

"Yes. Do you like it? Do you think it's too much?"

"I don't think it's too much at all, and yes, I love it." I smiled. "Think about what you want for dinner and we'll order in before we decorate the tree."

"Already done." She grinned as she led me into the kitchen, where the table was set with plates and a large pizza box sat in the center of the table. "I hope you don't mind. I was craving pizza."

"Not at all, baby. Pizza sounds good." I leaned over and kissed her.

After we ate, I put on some Christmas music and we decorated the tree. It was a beautiful evening and reminded me of the time we decorated her tree together all those years ago.

"It's beautiful," Quinn said as she stood back and placed her hands over her mouth.

"It is beautiful. By the way, my dad happened to go to Kingston's today and noticed the tree was missing." I gave a playful smirk.

"Oh no. Was he mad?"

"No. Not at all. I told him the tree looked better here anyway. I have something for you."

"You do?" A bright smile crossed her lips.

"Go sit down on the couch. I'll be right back." I walked over to my briefcase that was sitting in the foyer, opened it up, took out the small box, and handed it to her.

"I was going to give this to you for Christmas, but I thought you should have it now."

"Noah, I can wait."

"Maybe you can, but I can't."

She slowly lifted the lid.

"Is this?" she asked as she looked at me.

"It is." I smiled. "I had it repaired. It's yours and you should have it."

She lightly ran her finger over the heart-shaped locket before taking it out of the box.

"I will always love you to the moon and back," I said.

Her eyes began to water, and she wrapped her arms tightly around my neck.

"I love you so much. Thank you for this."

"You're welcome, baby. Let me put it on you."

I took the necklace from her and placed it around her neck.

"There. It's right back where it belongs," I spoke as I kissed her soft lips.

"Stay right here." She smiled. "I'm going to get my camera."

She ran up the stairs and back down with her camera and tripod. After she set it up, she told me to go stand in front of the tree. She set the timer and joined me.

"Smile," she spoke. "I have it set to take multiple shots, so keep smiling."

❧

Christmas Day

FOR THE FIRST TIME IN TWELVE YEARS, I WAS HAPPY TO WAKE UP ON Christmas morning. Quinn and I spent Christmas Eve with my family, including my aunts, uncles, and cousins. Today, my parents, Ellen and her husband, Todd, Henry, and Dr. Cooper were joining us at our home. Quinn stirred as she lay tightly against me and I softly stroked her beautiful brown hair.

"Merry Christmas, baby," I spoke, and she opened her eyes.

"Merry Christmas." Her smile lit up the room as she lifted her head and brought her lips up to mine.

We climbed out of bed and went into the kitchen to grab some coffee before we opened our presents. One of my gifts from Quinn was a framed photo collage of some of the pictures she took of us together for my desk.

"Aw, baby. I love it. I love us." I grinned as I leaned over and gave her a kiss.

She loved the diamond earrings and the Coco Chanel handbag and matching wallet I had bought her.

"Thank you for my gifts. I love them." Her lips met mine.

"You're welcome. I think you should go check your stocking." The corners of my mouth curved upwards.

"I thought we agreed that we weren't going to put anything in each other's stockings."

"It's no big deal. It's just something small. I saw it and couldn't help myself."

🐾 25 🐾

Q*uinn*
  "You first." I grinned as I handed him his stocking.
  "Really?" He cocked his head as he took it from me.
"I should say the same to you, mister."

He reached into his stocking and pulled out two playoff tickets. As he held them in his hand, he stared at me in shock.

"How did you get these? It's been sold out for months."

"I have connections." I grinned. "Take Henry and have fun."

"He's going to shit when I show him these. Quinn, I couldn't even get the tickets."

"I have my ways." I gave him a wink.

"You are the best girlfriend in the world." He wrapped his arms around me and hugged me tight."

He got up, took my stocking from the mantel, and handed it to me. With a smile, I reached inside, all the way to the bottom, and pulled out a small box. A fluttering sensation flowed through me as my heart started pounding and I slowly opened the lid. Inside the pretty box was the most beautiful diamond ring I'd ever seen in my life. I was speechless. Noah took the box from my hand, took out the ring, and inhaled a deep breath.

"Quinn, my best friend, my lover, and my queen. You are the love of my life, past, present, and future. Will you marry me?"

Tears swelled in my eyes as he held the ring up to me.

"Yes, Noah Kingston, I will marry you!"

With a smile, he placed the ring on my finger and our lips mingled together with our first kiss as a newly engaged couple.

Suddenly, there was a knock at the door.

"Who on earth is here this early?" I asked.

"I don't know. I'll go see. Why don't you go in the kitchen and make us some more coffee?"

"Okay." I smiled as I kissed his lips one more time.

I stared at the gorgeous ring that sat upon my finger all the way to the kitchen. As I popped a k-cup into the Keurig machine, I heard Noah walk into the kitchen. When I turned around, I stood in shock when I saw my grandmother standing there.

"Merry Christmas, Quinn."

"Oh my god, I can't believe you're here." I walked over and gave her a hug. "Merry Christmas."

I hadn't spoken to her since that day I left her home in Minnesota.

"You never returned any of my calls," I said.

"Because I was so ashamed of what I'd done. I didn't think you'd ever forgive me. You have an amazing man here." She placed her hand on Noah's arm. "I'm so sorry I didn't realize it back then. It's just the two of you were so young and—"

"You don't have to say another word, Grandma. The only thing that matters is you're here with us." I smiled. "Look." I held out my hand. "Noah asked me to marry him and I said yes."

She glanced up at Noah with a smile on her face.

"Wait a minute. You already knew?" I asked her.

"Your future husband came to Minnesota to ask for my blessing."

"What?" I cocked my head at him. "You told me you were going to Chicago for a business meeting."

"Well, I couldn't very well tell you I was going to see your grand-mother, could I?"

"You asked her to come here, didn't you?"

"He did. We had a lovely chat and I couldn't have picked a better or more respectable man than him for my granddaughter. I'm assuming you're cooking."

"I am." I smiled. "Noah wanted to hire a chef and I told him no. I wanted to cook."

"Then I'm helping you," my grandmother said. "It'll be just like old times."

"I'm so happy you're here."

"Me too, honey." She placed her hand on my cheek.

Christmas was celebrated with family and friends, and after everyone left, Noah and I headed upstairs to bed. I was in the bathroom taking off my makeup and Noah was changing out of his clothes in the bedroom. I stopped what I was doing, dropped the washcloth, gripped the edge of the bathroom counter, and stared at myself in the mirror.

"Baby, are you okay?" Noah asked as he walked into the bathroom.

I couldn't answer him.

"Quinn?" He walked over and gripped my shoulders from behind, staring at me in the mirror as I stared back.

"We're going to have the grandest wedding of all. We'll get married in Central Park at the prettiest spot and then we'll have an elegant reception at the Plaza Hotel, where everything will be decorated in pink and gold. Our wedding will be the most talked about wedding in New York City."

He gripped my shoulders tight and swallowed hard as I watched tears spring to his eyes through the mirror.

"Quinn. Those were the same exact words you spoke before the accident. How—"

"I don't know." I turned around and faced him. "It was just something that came to me. I can't explain it."

He pulled me in, and I wrapped my arms around him as he held my head against his chest.

"That's all I know," I softly spoke.

"It doesn't matter. My god, it doesn't matter." He kissed the top of my head.

❧ 26 ❧

Q uinn
The next morning, Noah left for the office and I sat
at the island with my hands wrapped around the warm
mug of coffee, thinking about last night and the small memory I had.
Noah told me it was a good sign, but I shouldn't keep thinking about it
because I'd ultimately drive myself crazy. He didn't understand. He
couldn't, and I didn't blame him for that. Missing five years of my life
wasn't something that I could just forget about. It wasn't something
that I could sweep under the rug and pretend it never happened. I
never forgot about it once since the accident. Sure, I moved on with
my life, but it stayed with me and on my mind every single day of my
life. And now that I'd met him and found out we were in love before
everything happened, it only heightened my need to remember.

I got dressed, grabbed my purse, and hailed a cab.

"Where to?" the cab driver asked.

I rattled off the address and let out a sigh. My phone dinged, and
when I pulled it from my purse, there was a text message from Noah.

*"Hey, baby. Heading into a meeting and I'll be unavailable for most of the
day. What are you up to today?"*

"Hi. I'm just running a few errands and checking out the after Christmas sales. Can I pick you up anything?"

"I already have everything I need. I love you to the moon and back."

"I love you too, Noah."

"Enjoy the rest of your day, baby. I'll see you later tonight."

"I can't wait."

Just as the cab pulled up to the curb, a car pulled into the driveway.

"Hi." An over-exuberant redheaded woman in a black pants suit smiled as she climbed out of her car. "Are you here for the open house?"

Open house?

I glanced over and noticed the for sale sign that sat on the lawn.

"Yes. Yes I am." I smiled as I climbed out of the cab.

"Great. Follow me inside." She waved her hand. "I'm sorry I'm running a little late. I have a sick child at home and finding a babysitter on such short notice isn't exactly easy."

"I totally understand and I hope your child feels better soon."

"You are so sweet. Thank you." She smiled.

I slowly walked up the steps to the porch while she inserted the key into the lock. The same steps I walked up and down thousands of times. We both stepped inside the house, and I could feel the air in my lungs constrict around me.

"Where are my manners? I'm Vicky Larson, the realtor who's handling the sale of this lovely house." She extended her well-manicured hand.

"I'm Quinn Reid." I placed my hand in hers. I didn't think it was wise to tell her my real last name.

"Nice to meet you, Quinn. So are you and your husband looking to buy?"

"My fiancé and I are." I smiled as I held up my hand. "Not quite married yet."

"Well, you've picked the perfect home to look at. This home is built for a newlywed couple and it's the perfect house to raise a family in. Here's the brochure with some information about the house. Shall I show you around?"

"Thank you. But if you don't mind, I'd like to take a look around myself. I really want to absorb it all in."

"Of course. I'll be in the kitchen if you have any questions." She grinned.

I grabbed on to the railing and slowly walked up the stairs. The one thing I noticed was that all the wood floors were exactly the same as I remembered them when I was twelve. I reached the top of the stairs and turned to the left where my bedroom was. Walking inside, I inhaled a sharp breath as I stared at the empty space before me. I smiled as visions of pink walls, white furniture, and a dollhouse in the corner filled my mind. The same dollhouse that my dad used to sit at and play with me. I walked over to the window and looked out at the backyard where I used to swing on a tire tied to the oak tree that was still standing tall and proud. When I stepped over to where my bed used to sit, I noticed a creak in the floorboard. I stepped away and then stepped on it again with a smile. My father always meant to fix that. I guess he never got around to it. Bending down, I ran my finger along edges of the board and slowly lifted it up. Glancing underneath, I saw a blue book with the word "Diary" imprinted in white. Picking it up, I looked and saw a gold lock dangling from it. Damn it. My heart started racing at the thought that it could be mine. But there was no way it would still be here after all these years. I shoved the diary in my purse and headed down the stairs.

"Excuse me, Vicky, there's a creaky floorboard in one of the bedrooms."

"I know." She smiled. "The previous owners had a teenage daughter when they moved in and didn't bother to fix it because they considered it their alarm. It would let them know if their daughter was sneaking in and out at all hours of the night."

"Well, kids are smart and I'm sure she found a way to get around it," I said.

"I'm sure you're right. So what did you think about the house?"

"It's lovely. I will talk to my fiancé about it and maybe bring him by for a look."

"Excellent. Let me give you my card."

She handed me her business card with a smile and I thanked her for letting me see the house. Walking out the front door, I stopped for a minute and looked down at the steps. Little did I know that when I walked out of the house that night, it would be the last time I'd ever walk up and down those steps again. I climbed into the cab that was waiting for me at the curb and had him drive me home.

⚜

I WENT INTO NOAH'S OFFICE AND TOOK TWO PAPERCLIPS FROM HIS desk. Taking them and the diary upstairs, I sat down on the bed and attempted to pop the lock. If the previous owners had a teenage daughter, then I was sure this diary belonged to her. I honestly couldn't think of a reason why I'd hide a diary. My parents weren't nosy people and they would never invade my privacy. At least when I was twelve, they wouldn't have. Who knew, maybe they changed, and as I became a teenager, they snooped around my room. God, I hated not remembering.

I played with the paperclips and the lock until I successfully opened it. My heart was pounding out of my chest as I slowly opened to the first page. I had no clue if it was mine or not. The pages spoke of school, friends, boys, sports events that were attended, hot teachers, and a first kiss with a guy named Neil. I let out a long sigh as I thumbed through the pages. As I got towards the back of the diary, I stumbled across a page that caught my attention and brought a smile to my face.

Dear Diary, I met the hottest boy today at the store. His name is Noah Kingston and he asked me to go to dinner with him tonight. I've never met anyone like him before. The moment our eyes met, there was something inside his that felt like home. Am I crazy for saying that about someone I just met? He's taking me to dinner tonight and I can't wait to see him again.

Every page after that was only about him.

Dear Diary, Noah asked me to be his girlfriend and I happily said yes. He gave me a beautiful silver heart bracelet with the initials N & Q engraved on it and told me that he loved me. We had sex for the first time tonight in his bedroom. Every girl gets nervous their first time and all of my friends told me that the first time with a guy is the worst. But for me it wasn't. It was magical.

We took it very slow and he made me feel safe and comfortable. Afterwards, he held me in his arms and kept asking me if I was okay. He was so attentive and gentle. I will never forget that night and our first time.

Dear Diary, I have to pen these feelings that are inside of me. This is Noah's and my last summer together before he goes off to Yale. I'm scared to death for him to leave. I love him so much and I don't want anything to change between us. He is the best thing that had ever happened to me and the thought of distance coming between us scares the shit out of me. He told me that nothing will ever come between us and to stop worrying about it. But nothing is ever guaranteed. Life happens, and in a split second, things could change. I talked to my mom about how I felt and she told me that if the two of us were meant to be together forever, then nothing could ever tear us apart. As many fears as I have, I know deep in my heart and soul that the love we share would conquer all.

Dear Diary, Tonight was Noah's prom and he looked as handsome as ever in his tuxedo. It was a lot of fun as we ate great food and danced the night away. His friends were throwing an after prom party, but we didn't go. Noah wanted to spend the evening alone, so we went to Central Park, laid a blanket down on the grass, held hands, and talked about future as we looked up at the stars in the sky. We talked about marriage, where we wanted to live, the type of house we wanted to live in, and how many kids we wanted to have. He wants three and I want two. But because I love him so much, I'd give him whatever he wants.

Dear Diary, today Noah and I are going to spend the day in Central Park and I'm bringing my camera and taking a million pictures of him and us. I want to make him a collage for when he goes off to Yale. He doesn't know about it and I'm going to give it to him the day he leaves. I wish I could just rewind and go back to the day we first met. Gotta go...Noah is here and waiting downstairs for me. I'll write more later...

I sat there reading the pages as tears streamed down my face. That was the last entry I made. Was that the day of the accident?

I heard the front door open, so I hid the diary in the drawer of the nightstand and went downstairs.

❧ 27 ❧

Noah
I stepped inside the penthouse, set down my briefcase, and loosened my tie. Quinn came running down the stairs and wrapped her arms around me.

"What's that for?" I laughed.

"I'm so happy you're home. I missed you."

"I missed you too, baby." I kissed her lips. "How was your day?"

"It was good. How was yours?"

"Stressful. But all that stress is gone now that I'm home with you." I kissed the tip of her nose. "I'm starving. What do you want to do for dinner?"

"I want to order in and stay wrapped in your arms on the couch."

"I love that idea. I'm going to go upstairs and change. Decide what you want to eat."

"I'll order us some Chinese if that's what you want," she spoke.

"Chinese sounds good."

"I'll order it now." She smiled. "And I'll pour us some wine."

After splashing some cold water on my face and changing into comfortable clothes, I went downstairs and found Quinn sitting on the couch with our wine glasses. I sat down next to her and wrapped my arm around her as she cuddled into me with her legs up on the couch.

"Noah?" she asked.

"What is it, baby?" I took a sip of wine.

"What did we do the day of the accident?"

"We spent the day together in Central Park. Why?"

"I was just wondering."

"Did you have another memory?"

"No. I just want to know how we spent our last day together."

"We went to Central Park and you took an obscene amount of pictures of me and of us. Every time I turned around, you had that camera pointed at me." I smiled. "Then I gave you the locket and it started to pour down rain out of nowhere. So I grabbed your hand and we ran and hid under Greyshot Arch until it stopped. Then I took you home, took that picture of you and your parents, kissed you goodbye, and then I left."

The penthouse phone rang to alert us that our food had arrived. After answering the door and tipping the delivery boy, I took the food into the kitchen and set it on the table. I was a little concerned as to why Quinn had asked me about the day of the accident.

"Are you sure there isn't a reason why you wanted to know about that day?" I asked.

She looked at me as tears filled her eyes, and suddenly, I became worried.

"Quinn, what is it? What's wrong?"

"Nothing is wrong," she spoke as she wiped the tear that fell down her face. "Everything is right."

"Baby, I have no clue what you're talking about."

"Sit down and start eating. I'll be right back."

I sighed as I took a seat at the table and opened up the container of kung pao chicken. A few moments later, she returned, and it appeared she was hiding something behind her back. I didn't say a word as I let her speak.

"I went back to my old house today. I just thought maybe if I was there, it would trigger some sort of memory. When I was released from the hospital, my grandmother took me straight to the airport.

She had gone to the house and packed all my things. She wouldn't let me go back there. She said it would have been too painful for me. When I got to the house, it just so happened that the house is up for sale and there was an open house. I met the realtor and took a look around. I went upstairs to my bedroom and there was always this one floorboard that creaked."

"I remember that damn board." I smiled.

"I don't know why I did this, but I ran my finger along the edges of it and lifted it up. When I removed the floorboard, I found this hiding inside."

She removed her hand from behind her back, handed me a diary, and then took the seat across from me at the table.

"Is this yours?" I asked.

"I wasn't sure at first because it was locked. So when I got home, I popped the lock with a couple paper clips and I started reading it. I still wasn't sure because all that was written was about school and friends." She took the diary from my hand, opened to a specific page, and handed it back to me. "Then I saw this page and I knew this was my diary. Go ahead, read it."

I sat there reading with her diary in one hand and a fork in the other, reading each entry as I ate my kung pao chicken. I looked up at her as she sat there with a smile and tears streaming down her face.

"You wrote about our time together."

"I know." She nodded her head. "A lot of it's all there. And now I do have those memories because I wrote about it, and I read it, and it's in my memory."

I pursed my lips and lightly shook my head as I got up from my chair and walked over to her.

"I can't believe this," I said as she stood up and I wrapped my arms around her, hugging her tight.

"I can put that part of my life to rest," she whispered. "I finally have my closure."

❦ 28 ❦

EIGHT MONTHS LATER

uinn

Q I stood in front of the three-way mirror and stared at myself in the beautiful Vera Wang strapless Cinderella ball gown wedding dress embellished with Swarovski crystals. My long brown locks were placed in an elegant updo, where a cathedral veil, which was also embellished with Swarovski crystals, sat upon my head.

"You are absolutely stunning," my grandmother said as she wiped her eyes.

"Thanks, Grandma."

She took hold of my hand and gave it a gentle squeeze.

"Quinn, it's time," Marcy, our wedding planner, spoke.

As much as Noah and I wanted to get married in Central Park, it couldn't accommodate the number of guests that wanted to see us get married, so we decided to have the ceremony under the canopy at the Plaza Hotel. After the ceremony, while our guests were enjoying cocktails and appetizers, Noah and I would take a carriage ride through Central Park.

I hooked my arm around my grandmother's, and we made our way to the top of the aisle, where Noah's father was waiting. Both of them were going to walk me down to my fiancé.

"You look simply gorgeous, Quinn." Grant smiled.

"Thanks, Dad." I smiled back.

The music started to play and the only thing I could see walking down the aisle was my future husband staring back at me with a bright smile across his face. As soon as I approached him, both my grandmother and Grant took my hand and placed it in Noah's.

Noah

THE MOMENT I SAW HER WALK DOWN THE AISLE, SHE TOOK MY breath away. More so now than ever before. My heart started to pick up its beat as she walked towards me. I shouldn't have been nervous, but I was. I stood there with my hands cupped in front of me and a smile on my face. As soon as she approached, I took her hand in mine. We were supposed to immediately turn to the minister, but instead, I ran the back of my hand down her cheek.

"You look stunningly beautiful."

"And you look incredibly handsome."

"I love you."

"I love you too."

We turned to the minister, who spoke a few words, and then it was time for our vows. Vows that we wrote for each other.

"My beautiful bride." I smiled as I stared into her baby blue eyes. "The fact that the two of us are standing here, in this very spot, is a miracle. I never thought I'd see you again, but here you are, the love of my life who is about to become my wife. I vow to love you for eternity, and I promise to always take care of you. You are my best friend, my soulmate, my universe, and I vow to cherish you for the rest of our lives. I will always love you to the moon and back."

She stood there, tightening the grip on my hands as a single tear fell from her eyes.

"Noah, my best friend, my lover, and my one and only soulmate. I knew the moment I saw you that there was something special about you. I felt it the moment I looked into your eyes. For twelve years, I felt like a puzzle with a missing piece. Then I met you again and you fit perfectly into my world. You were my missing piece. The love we share is beyond measure. A love so strong that not even me losing my memory and what we had could keep us apart. I vow to love you for the rest of my life, and I vow to cherish and respect you til death do us part. I love you with my heart and soul and I always will."

I took my thumb and gently wiped the tears that fell from her eyes.

"That was beautiful," the minister spoke. "Noah, place this ring on Quinn's finger and repeat after me.

"With this ring, I thee wed."

I slipped the ring on her delicate finger and softly spoke with a smile upon my lips.

"With this ring, I thee wed."

"Quinn, place this ring on Noah's finger and repeat after me."

"With this ring, I thee wed."

She took hold of my hand and slid the band on my finger.

"With this ring, I thee wed." The corners of her mouth curved up into a beautiful smile.

"I now pronounce you husband and wife. You may kiss your bride, Noah," the minister spoke.

Quinn wrapped her arms around my neck as I placed mine around her waist and pulled her closer to me while we shared our first kiss as husband and wife. Our guests cheered and clapped for us and the music began to play. Taking Quinn's hand, we walked up the aisle and out the door to where a white carriage and white horses waited for us.

"Every year on our anniversary, I'm going to take you somewhere and we're going to renew our wedding vows," I spoke as we rode through Central Park.

"Every year?" She laughed. "I like that idea." She leaned over and kissed my cheek.

❧ 29 ❧

ONE YEAR LATER

N*oah*
      "Baby, are you ready? We're going to be late for our appointment."

"I'm coming," she spoke as she walked down the stairs. "I thought morning sickness was supposed to be over with by now."

"It'll pass soon." I held out my hand and she placed hers in mine.

Sean pulled up to the medical building and I helped Quinn out of the car. We stepped inside and took the elevator up to the second floor where her OB/GYN office was located. Today was the day of her ultrasound and the day we'd get to see our baby for the first time.

"Hello, you two." Dr. Corbett smiled as she walked in the room. "Are you ready to see your baby?"

"We've been ready since the day Quinn found out she was pregnant." I smiled.

"Well, let's not keep you waiting any longer."

Dr. Corbett squeezed some gel on Quinn's belly and placed the wand over it. Quinn gently squeezed my hand as the baby appeared on the screen. Dr. Corbett wasn't saying a word, and suddenly, I became very worried.

"Dr. Corbett, is everything okay?" Quinn asked in a frightened voice.

"Hold on a second, but there's nothing to be worried about," she spoke as she leaned closer to the ultrasound machine. "I'll be damned." She looked at us with a smile. "See this right here?" She pointed to something on the screen that we couldn't quite make out.

"What is that?" I asked.

"That's an arm."

"What do you mean? Our baby has three arms?!" Quinn went into panic mode.

"No. Oh my god, no. That's another baby. Congratulations, you two, you're having twins."

"Twins?" I spoke as my eyes widened.

"The sibling is hiding behind the other one. That's why we could only hear one heartbeat."

"We're having twins, Noah." Quinn's eyes filled with tears as she looked up at me.

"Yeah, baby, we are, and I couldn't be any happier." I smiled as I kissed her forehead.

☙❦❧

Six months later, Ella and Elijah Kingston were born into the world. Now I had three loves of my life: my wife, my daughter, and my son. Every day that I held them in my arms, I was reminded that second chances in life did indeed exist. From the day I walked out of Quinn's hospital room all those years ago, all I wanted to do was rewind time and get back what I had lost. But in the end, I didn't lose anything at all. I gained more than I ever thought possible.

ONE NIGHT IN PARIS

Coming Soon

CHAPTER ONE

Anna

Each of my bridesmaids gave me a hug and left the bridal room to go take their places. A few moments after they left, there was a light knock on the door, and when I opened it, my best friend, Franco, stood there holding my veil.

"Your veil." He grinned as he stared at me from head to toe. "You look absolutely beautiful, Anna."

"Thank you. Get in here!" I smiled as I pulled him inside the room.

I stood in front of the three-way mirror and stared at my reflection.

"You really outdid yourself with my wedding dress," I spoke to him.

"You deserve only the best, my dear." He smiled as he placed the veil he made on my head. "Are you okay?"

"Yeah. I'm fine," I hesitantly spoke.

I walked to the balcony and stared out at my future husband waiting for me with approximately two hundred guests who had properly taken their seats. The sun was shining brightly, for there wasn't a cloud in the sky. It was the perfect day to get married.

Franco took hold of my hand and lightly gripped it as he stood next to me.

"You don't have to do this. There is always plan B."

"I know. I better get down there. I'm late and my dad's going to kill me."

He let go of my hand, held out his arm, and walked me to the back of the hotel and down the stairs where my father waited for me.

"You're late," my father said as I took hold of his arm. "That is disrespectful to Matthew and your guests, Anna."

"Franco had to fix a button on my dress that came loose."

The music started to play, and I took in a deep breath. My stomach was tied in knot after knot walking down the white runner as every single guest stared at me with smiles upon their faces and bright flashes going off from their cameras. This was what was expected of me. But the thing was, I was never good at doing the expected. I stared at my future husband as he stared back at me. Even his stare was annoying. We were almost to the end of the aisle, when I came to an abrupt stop. It was now or never. I chose now.

"I'm sorry, Dad," I spoke as I turned to him and placed my hand on his cheek.

"Anna?"

I turned around, kicked off my heels, and ran up the aisle, throwing my wedding bouquet behind me with a smile on my face. I heard both my father and Matthew shouting my name, but I ignored them and kept running. I ran up the steps and into the hotel, through the lobby, and out the front door, climbing into the black limo that was parked along the curb.

"So you did it." Terrance, my driver smiled.

"I did it. Thanks for waiting for me, even though I wasn't sure."

"Not a problem, Anna. Airport?"

"Yes." I smiled.

۞

Freedom and exhilaration soared through me as the plane took off from LAX. I was on a high, something I always got when I was defiant. I was a strong-willed, independent woman, and when someone told me to do something, I always did the opposite. I'm not going to lie,

Matthew wasn't the love of my life. Why did I accept his marriage proposal? Because it was what my father wanted. I thought for once I'd grown up and I could make him proud. He brought Matthew into the company to groom him and to run it with me one day. That was how we met. He was practically shoved down my throat every single day. So I decided to go on a date with him. He was a decent guy, good-looking, and the rest is history. He grew on me, but I wasn't happy for the last year. I just went with the flow, worked, and planned my wedding. The way he kissed my father's ass was annoying. In fact, everything he did was annoying. Even the sex with him was annoying. I faked more orgasms than I had real ones. I gave *myself* better orgasms than what he could give me.

The plane touched down in Paris, and as soon as I turned on my phone, there were numerous text messages and missed calls from my father, with the exception of one text message from Franco.

"I knew you'd do it. Call me when you get to Paris, regardless of the time."

I took a cab to the Peninsula, where reservations were made for Mr. & Mrs. Matthew Brookes. Yep. I did it. I took our honeymoon anyway. I loved Paris and I needed the escape until things back home blew over.

"Bonjour." The man behind the desk smiled.

"Bonjour. Reservations for Brookes," I spoke.

"I'm sorry, Mrs. Brookes, but that reservation was cancelled yesterday."

I rolled my eyes. "Of course it was. And for the record, I never became Mrs. Brookes. I left my fiancé at the altar and I'm still Anna Young. So, since my honeymoon suite was cancelled, I'm going to need a room. The Garden Rooftop suite, if available."

"I'm sorry, Miss Young, but that suite is booked. I can put you in our Katara Suite."

"The Katara Suite will be fine." I smiled.

"Very good. I'll have someone bring up your bags."

I took the elevator up to the sixth floor, and as I was sliding my keycard to unlock the door, I noticed an incredibly sexy man walking out of the Rooftop Garden Suite next door.

"So you're the one who took my suite." I smirked as he passed by.

"Excuse me?" He stopped and turned around.

"Nothing. It was a joke. I just flew in and I wanted that suite and they told me that it was already booked."

"Well, we could always share it if you want it that badly." A sly smile crossed his perfectly handsome face.

"I'm sure your wife wouldn't appreciate that."

"I'm not married."

"Oh. Well, then, your girlfriend wouldn't appreciate it."

"No girlfriend either. It's just me in there. So you're welcome to join me." A smirk formed on his lips.

"I'm good with this suite but thank you for the offer." I blushed.

"If you change your mind, you know where to find me. I need to run. I'm late for a meeting." He smiled.

I sighed as I watched his six-foot-two stature and fine ass walk down the hallway in his tailored designer dark gray suit that fit him perfectly in all the right places. His brown hair was kept short all the way around with a slightly longer top, which had a wavy texture to it, and his rich brown eyes were captivating as they held me in a trance. In fact, every feature on his face was captivating. Damn, that man was sexy.

I opened the door to my suite and stepped inside with a smile on my face.

"Welcome to Paris, Anna," I spoke as I looked around.

BOOKS BY SANDI LYNN

If you haven't already done so, please check out my other books. Escape from reality and into the world of romance. I'll take you on a journey of love, pain, heartache and happily ever afters.

Millionaires:

The Forever Series (Forever Black, Forever You, Forever Us, Being Julia, Collin, A Forever Christmas, A Forever Family)

Love, Lust & A Millionaire (Wyatt Brothers, Book 1)

Love, Lust & Liam (Wyatt Brothers, Book 2)

Lie Next To Me (A Millionaire's Love, Book 1)

When I Lie with You (A Millionaire's Love, Book 2)

Then You Happened (Happened Series, Book 1)

Then We Happened (Happened Series, Book 2)

His Proposed Deal

A Love Called Simon

The Seduction of Alex Parker

Something About Lorelei

One Night In London

The Exception

Corporate A$$

A Beautiful Sight

The Negotiation

Defense

Playing The Millionaire

#Delete

Behind His Lies

Carter Grayson (Redemption Series, Book One)

ABOUT THE AUTHOR

Sandi Lynn is a New York Times, USA Today and Wall Street Journal bestselling author who spends all her days writing. She published her first novel, *Forever Black*, in February 2013 and hasn't stopped writing since. Her addictions are shopping, going to the gym, romance novels, coffee, chocolate, margaritas, and giving readers an escape to another world.

Be a part of my tribe and make sure to sign up for my news-letter so you don't miss a Sandi Lynn book again!

Facebook: www.facebook.com/Sandi.Lynn.Author
   Twitter: www.twitter.com/SandilynnWriter
   Website: www.authorsandilynn.com
   Pinterest: www.pinterest.com/sandilynnWriter
   Instagram: www.instagram.com/sandilynnauthor
   Goodreads: http://bit.ly/2w6tN25
   Newsletter: http://eepurl.com/bcPXRb

CPSIA information can be obtained
at www.ICGtesting.com
Printed in the USA
LVHW081424140420
653409LV00007B/263